Russia Girl

A Natalia Nicolaeva Thriller

Kenneth Rosenberg

Copyright 2019 by Kenneth Rosenberg
All Rights Reserved
www.kennethrosenberg.com

Also by Kenneth Rosenberg

Vendetta Girl – Natalia Nicolaeva #2
Enemies: A War Story
No Cure for the Broken Hearted
Memoirs of a Starving Artist
The Extra: A Hollywood Romance
Bachelor Number Five
Bachelor Number Nine
The Art of Love

Chapter One

Three women swung battered scythes at undulating stalks of grain, oblivious to shifting patterns of shadow and light all around them. They wore scarves on their heads and dresses made from cotton smoothed by years in sun and wind and rain. Ivanka, the matriarch, was a stocky, determined woman, who hacked at the wheat with a vengeance. Nineteen-year-old Natalia Nicolaeva was tall and lithe, with arms whose grace belied their strength. Rita, her sixteen-year-old sister, struggled with her smaller frame not yet grown into the task.

On better days, this work was done by an ancient heap of metal and bolts that passed for a combine harvester. Today was not one of those days. From where they worked, the women heard occasional grunts and curses from Victor, Natalia's father, as he struggled to repair the machine. What few animals they owned needed to be fed, and the grain brought in, so in the meantime, the women toiled the old-fashioned way. Natalia didn't mind the work so much. It took her mind off their troubles and it made her strong, though she worried about her sister who pushed herself so hard.

"Rita, don't wear yourself out," said Natalia.

"What's wrong, you can't keep up?!" Rita countered crossly, determined to do her share.

"We'll all stop," said their mother, throwing her scythe to the ground, "and load the cart." Ivanka walked to their fifty-year-old tractor, with peeling red paint and a wooden cart attached to the back. She launched herself up and into the seat and turned the ignition. The engine sputtered and came to life. With head raised high and lips pursed tightly in a stern expression of fortitude, the girls' mother wheeled the tractor around beside the freshly cut wheat before climbing down to help her daughters scoop the stalks into their arms and then pile them on the cart.

"You don't have to be so curt with me," an annoyed Natalia said to her little sister.

"If I wanted your opinion I'd ask for it," Rita countered.

"You're a Nicolaeva, that's for sure," said Natalia. "A real pain in the ass."

"I learned from the best," said Rita.

"Quiet you two!" commanded their mother.

Rita and Natalia looked at each other with vexed expressions as they continued piling their load.

When the day grew long and the animals were fed, Natalia's body ached with exhaustion. Inside the family's modest farmhouse, she used a bucket and a rag to wash herself in a large porcelain bathtub and then quickly changed into jeans and a well-worn sweater. It was Thursday, her night to meet Sonia for dinner in the village. When she was dressed and ready, she slid her phone into her pocket and took the keys to the family's rusted Lada from a peg near the door. "I'll be back in a few hours." Natalia ducked out, bounding down the front steps and on past a wooden corral, where two sway-backed horses munched freshly cut hay. In another enclosure, three pigs lounged lazily in the dirt. The lone milk cow was ensconced in the barn for the night. Smoke from a cooking fire drifted up from the chimney of the small house where Natalia's sister-in-law Olga lived with her three young children. Inside, they would just be sitting down to dinner themselves. Natalia paused, tempted to duck in for a visit with her niece and nephews; especially Constantine, who always had a smile for her, even when chronic asthma kept him confined to his bed. There was a lesson to be learned from this plucky four-year-old. His undying enthusiasm tugged at her heartstrings. She *should* stop in to kiss the children goodnight, but she was already running late. Natalia opened the door to the Lada and climbed in. She turned the key and pressed lightly on the gas pedal. The engine coughed twice and then rumbled to life. This car was falling apart on the outside but her father kept the mechanics in good order. Natalia drove up and over a low hill and then continued down the dirt track that led toward the highway.

"Why does he have to come here?" Sonia muttered under her breath. She was a pretty, heavyset girl with ivory white skin. Her round face was framed by smooth dark hair. On her lips, she wore bright red lipstick. Sonia's eyes narrowed as she scowled in the direction of Gregor Multinovic, who sat eating at a table on the sidewalk just outside.

"He pays his bill, doesn't he?" Standing beside her friend in the back of the restaurant, Natalia turned around to look.

"He scares away the other customers." Sonia was the only waitress at her mother's establishment, where the pair of them served meals six days a week and lived together upstairs. "Look at this place. It's empty but for him! Besides, he scares me, too."

"He's just here to eat. Forget about it. Come here, my love!" Natalia gave her friend a kiss on each cheek.

"Oh, sit down," Sonia scoffed, "I'll bring something out."

Natalia chose a table where, through an open window, she could watch Multinovic quietly sipping from a bowl of soup. The man was at least twice Natalia's age, with bushy salt-and-pepper hair. He had a rugged look about him, with a strong chin and a weathered face. Not altogether unattractive, she had to admit. Natalia wondered if he gained pleasure from eating or if it was simply a means toward survival. She'd never seen the man smile. She wondered if he even knew how. Multinovic had arrived in Drosti several years before. He kept mostly to himself but the village was full of rumors about his dark and violent past. He was an arms dealer, drug dealer, war criminal, ex-mobster. He was a killer and a rapist, running from the law. Natalia believed that there must be something to the rumors. If not, then why was he here? This Serb hiding out in the no-man's land that was Transnistria? He might as well have disappeared off the face of the earth. As far as the local residents were concerned, Multinovic was the monster who one day came to town, and while nobody wanted him around, they were all too frightened to do anything about it. Natalia didn't realize she was staring until he swiveled his head abruptly, catching her in his withering gaze. Her eyes shifted downwards as she gripped tightly to her table. Sonia reappeared with two plates of pasta and two Coca Cola's. "What's wrong with *you*?" She placed the food and drinks on the table.

"What do you mean?" Natalia released her grip and eased her shoulders back, trying to hide her anxiety.

Sonia looked briefly toward Multinovic. "You think he's handsome, don't you?" She cracked a wry smile.

"What?!" Natalia recoiled. "Are you kidding?"

"Oh, come on," Sonia teased. "You can tell me."

Natalia laughed lightly. "You always did have an odd sense of humor."

After taking a seat, Sonia watched the man finishing his soup. "You have to admit, he does have a certain charisma. Not like the rest of the men around here."

"I thought you couldn't stand him?" Natalia tried not to raise her voice.

"You know he's a rapist, right?"

"All I know is rumors, just like you."

"Wouldn't you like to be raped by him? It might not be so bad, eh?"

"Sonia!" Natalia gasped. "I think you've officially lost your mind."

"That's what this village does to me. I'm a desperate woman."

"That much is true." Natalia sipped at her coke.

"Can you blame me?"

"No, I don't suppose I can…"

"So come with me, then."

"Come with you where?! What is it this time, Sonia?" Natalia had long ago grown tired of this conversation, repeated weekly.

"There's a woman, looking for waitresses. For a restaurant in Italy." Sonia challenged Natalia to argue with her.

"Great, then move to Italy," Natalia replied.

"Two waitresses, Natalia. I'm serious this time."

"I'm not interested."

"Come on! It's the opportunity we've always dreamed of! Why won't you listen at least?"

"Because they're *your* dreams, not mine!"

"They used to be *our* dreams."

"Well, they're not anymore."

Sonia put her elbows on the table and clasped her hands together. "I know this has something to do with Vitaly, but I'm talking about Italy! La dolce vita!"

Natalia shook her head. "It's not about Vitaly. My family needs me here. I'm not going anywhere, so you'd better get used to that fact."

"I don't care what you try to tell yourself, Natalia, there is no future for us in this place. Besides, think of the money you could send home! Think what good that would do for them!"

Natalia wanted to insist that Sonia was wrong about that last part, but in truth, she simply couldn't. No matter how stoic her parents tried to remain, Natalia understood what a tenuous life they led.

"What are you going to do, marry Vitaly, and then what? Spend the rest of your life here? Is that what you really want?"

"I just want to be left alone. That's all."

"My mother knows this woman," Sonia went on. "They went to school together. Svetlana lives in Odessa now, but she's home visiting family. She came by this morning and told me all about it."

Natalia's skepticism was apparent, though her fortitude was slipping. "Why Italy? If she lives in Odessa?"

"She knows people. Believe me, she's very nice. I promise. And the pay! Eight hundred euros per month! Or more! Imagine what we could do with that..."

Natalia looked down at her food. Her cheeks flushed a pale red as she tried to hide the conflicting emotions that swirled within her. It wasn't too long ago that she and Sonia plotted their escape from Drosti together, but that was before the disappearance of her brother, Leon. Natalia saw what losing their only son did to her parents, both emotionally and physically. The abandonment of his family marked their failure, at least in their own eyes. It also meant more work for everyone else, especially Olga, left to raise their children as a single mother. Natalia couldn't bring herself to leave them all behind as well. Things were sure to be better in Italy or elsewhere, but ever since Leon left, Natalia reluctantly resigned herself to staying put. Her parents had never been more than 100 km from Drosti. They accepted this place as their destiny. It was easier for them, though. For much of their lives, going abroad was simply not an option. Not under a communist regime fearful of an exodus to the West. Natalia was born into a free society, but with freedom came choices, and with choices came decisions. In some ways, the old life was a lot less complicated. You did as you were told. You accepted the circumstances you were born into. Things were simple. But those days were long over. Natalia had choices to make and no matter how much she tried to extinguish that fire of ambition, she knew it still burned inside her. If she let an opportunity like this pass her by, she might spend the rest of her life wondering, haunted by seeds of doubt and regret.

At the table outside, the girls saw Multinovic reach into his back pocket and pull out his wallet. He dropped some bills on the table and stood to go, but then stopped abruptly, turning to stare at them through the window. His mouth opened slightly, as though he were about to say something, but then thought better of it, furrowing his brow before walking briskly away down the sidewalk.

"Thank God," Sonia said with a shudder.

"I thought you wanted him to rape you?"

Sonia responded with an angry glare.

"You're the one who said it." Natalia picked up a fork and twirled it in her pasta.

"I just don't understand why he would come to Drosti of all places... Why would anyone *choose* to live here?"

"Is it really so bad?"

"Do I have to answer that?"

Natalia scowled. "He must have his reasons. Maybe you should ask him sometime."

"You think I want to have an actual conversation with that man?"

"You seem awfully curious about him."

"*Please*, Natalia."

"He can't be much worse than all of those fat Americans you write to, half a world away."

"They're not all fat," said Sonia. "Or American. Some of them are fat Australians. Or wrinkly old Norwegians." She laughed at her own joke. "Even *they* don't want to come here. Why would they?"

"Why would you want to marry some man you've never even met?"

"Natalia, you know how I feel. Every day it's like my soul is slowly being crushed in this place. I can't take it much more, I really can't."

Natalia breathed deeply. "Let's talk about something else for a while."

Sonia looked Natalia in the eye. "Just promise me you'll meet this woman, won't you? Svetlana. All you have to do is meet her."

Natalia screwed her face into a pained expression. "Fine, I'll meet her," she relented. "But I'm not promising anything else."

A light smile crossed Sonia's lips. "That's all I ask."

Chapter Two

Natalia left Sonia's house at dawn and drove back through the quiet streets, past the aging shops, wood-plank sidewalks and warped wooden homes beaten down by ruthless eastern winters. Fading yellow paint peeled from the Russian Orthodox Church, while the bulbous golden dome on top reflected the day's first thin rays of light. As she passed the school, Natalia remembered the terror she'd felt being dropped off there for the very first time. Yet while Drosti was little changed since that day, Natalia herself had grown beyond it. Despite her apprehensions, a part of her longed to fly far, far away, to leave the hopelessness and the pain and the despair of this place behind.

Of course, there was also Vitaly to consider. He'd be home from the army in a just a few more months. Everyone in the village expected them to get married, eventually. Even Natalia expected it. Part of her longed for the stability that represented. But did she love him? Natalia wasn't sure. Maybe in time she would, like her parents had grown to love each other.

Continuing along the single paved road out of town, Natalia watched as the countryside came to life for the day. Farmers hitched up horses or climbed aboard their own antiquated equipment and headed for the fields. She slowed behind an old tractor moving ahead of her down the road, recognizing Oleg behind the wheel, a neighbor with a shock of billowing gray hair. His was another ancient machine like her father's, becoming harder and harder to repair as the spare parts ceased to exist. Natalia tooted her horn as she passed and Oleg raised a hand in reply.

After a few more kilometers, Natalia turned left off the paved road and wound up and over rolling hills, through wheat fields and past small scraps of remnant forest. Thoughts of her future still swirled through her mind. Everyone had heard the stories about what happened to girls who went abroad. Nightmarish, terrible stories. But those things didn't happen to girls like Natalia. They happened to naïve girls who didn't know any better. Or girls of questionable morals, who put themselves in compromising situations. Sonia and Natalia were too smart for that. Right? She couldn't help but wonder. For the time being Natalia had her other things to worry about. First she had to milk the cow and collect some eggs from the chicken coop so that her niece and two young nephews could have their breakfast. Then she had to help again with the harvest, one way or another.

As she pulled up to the farmhouse, she saw their neighbor Vladimir talking to her father. Victor Nicolaev was a burly man, with a round face and large, bushy eyebrows. He kept mostly to himself and rarely said more than necessary. Some thought him gruff, but Natalia knew he was merely practical. Vladimir, the neighbor, was a skinny, energetic man who never seemed to stop moving. He'd pestered Natalia's father for years to join a local collective, but Victor was too proud. He was a slave to that system for most of his life. Now he wanted a farm of his own, to work by his own rules, only it seemed they were always one bad harvest away from disaster. Vladimir knew it only too well.

"Good morning, Natalia," said her father.

"Good morning." Natalia climbed from the car and then moved into the barn where she found the cow patiently waiting.

Chapter Three

As soon as she walked in the front door, Natalia felt as though she were on display. Eyeing her was a round woman dressed in a beige velour top and brown polyester pants, with an unnatural orange tint to her hair. She took a long draw on her cigarette and exhaled from the side of her mouth. She looked innocuous enough, like anybody's aunt or mother. Beside her at the table sat Sonia, across from her own mother, Raisa.

"Here she is!" Sonia beamed. "This is my Natalia."

"Hello." Natalia returned her own uneasy smile. She placed her phone and keys on the table and took a seat, trying to relax. It would be over soon enough.

"So, do you have any experience as a waitress?" the woman asked right off.

"Me? No. No, I don't." Natalia leaned back. Was this an interview, already?

"I don't suppose you speak any Italian, but that's ok, you'll learn. Some English would help. Do you speak any English?"

"I studied it in school." She turned to look at Raisa, who took a puff from her own cigarette but said nothing.

"Not that the Italians speak it, heaven forbid," the other woman continued, "but the tourists all do."

"This is Svetlana," Sonia cut in. "Her friend owns the restaurant I told you about."

"Yes, and where is this restaurant, exactly?" Natalia asked.

"It's a lovely little town in Italy. Brindisi, on the Adriatic Sea. You'll love it there. If we agree to have you."

"Natalia is a fast learner. And a hard worker," Sonia offered eagerly. "Look how strong she is. And how pretty!"

"Yes, she is a pretty girl," Svetlana conceded. "Cigarette?" she offered a pack.

"No, thank you," Natalia replied.

"And a healthy one, too. That's good."

"Who said I'd agreed to go with this anyway?" Natalia tried not to sound defensive.

"Why wouldn't you?" Svetlana was taken aback. "I thought that's why you came to see me?"

"I promised Sonia I'd speak to you. That's all."

"Don't you want to earn some money? Don't you want a better life?" Svetlana seemed offended.

"My life isn't so bad."

Svetlana took another drag on her cigarette and shrugged. "Suit yourself," she exhaled. An uncomfortable silence hung over the table.

"Svetlana lived in Drosti when she was a little girl." Sonia made an effort to break the impasse.

"Yes. I knew Raisa when we were children. Isn't that so, Raisa?"

Raisa nodded.

"And you've spent some time in Italy?" Natalia asked.

"I visit Italy quite frequently," said Svetlana.

"Her husband is a businessman," Sonia offered.

"And who is the owner of this restaurant?" said Natalia.

"This girl has many questions. Very good," said Svetlana. "She wants to know what she is getting herself into."

"Oh, no," Natalia shook her head. She refused to be manipulated. They couldn't suck her in against her will. This woman had the power to turn her life upside down. For the better, maybe, but then again maybe for the worse.

"Did I say something wrong?" Svetlana asked.

"Natalia doesn't want to leave her family," Sonia tried to explain.

"I see," said Svetlana. "You've never been away from home before? It's only natural you'd be a little worried. The world can be a frightening place."

"I have been away," Natalia countered.

"To Tiraspol," Sonia added.

"Tiraspol?!" Svetlana laughed. "Oh, honey… Tiraspol doesn't count."

"Even if I wanted to go with you, it's impossible. I don't have a passport. Besides, the Italians would never accept it anyway. Not from Transnistria."

"But Svetlana can help us get Moldovan passports!" said Sonia.

"That's right. I have a good connection in Chisinau. You just leave that to me."

Natalia lifted her keys and phone from the table. "I think I'd better be going. Thank you for your time." She glanced at Sonia briefly, noting the look of disappointment on her friend's face, and then bolted from the room.

Out on the sidewalk, Sonia caught up to Natalia before she'd opened the car door. "Tell me," Sonia said. "What do you want out of life?"

"I just want to be happy, like anyone," Natalia faced her. "And I want to be left alone."

"Are you happy? Because I don't think so. I think that your life is filled with sadness. I think you are resigned to this sadness, as though it was simply your fate, but you're wrong Natalia. Misery is not your fate!"

"Sonia, don't do this," Natalia pleaded.

"You're using your family as an excuse, just because you had one bad experience outside this place."

"That's not true."

"Tell me then, what do you think it will take to make you happy? Can you really find it here?"

"Why are you so sure that the key to happiness is leaving? The key to happiness is in here," Natalia touched her chest. "It is in learning to be content with what you have, not chasing after what you don't."

Sonia licked her lips and thought carefully about her response. "I know I'm not happy here and I never will be," she began. "Getting out is my only chance and I want you to come with me. We've been together our whole lives. Ever since we were little girls, clinging to our mothers skirts. Do you remember, the day that we first met?"

"Yes, I remember."

"Your mother brought you to meet me. She wanted you to have a friend. I can picture you here in the doorway, standing just behind her, trying to hide," Sonia laughed. "You were so shy back then."

"And you were so loud."

"I suppose things haven't changed so much, have they? Who would have thought we'd still be together, after all of these years?"

"So why insist that it end?"

"Please, Natalia, don't make me beg. If you don't like it in Italy you can always come home."

Natalia opened the door to the Lada and climbed in, dropping her phone on the passenger seat and placing the keys in the ignition. She gripped the steering wheel tightly with both hands and stared straight ahead. "I'll think about it."

"Do you mean that?"

"Do I have to say it again?" Natalia snapped.

Sonia could hardly contain her glee. "Just picture it! The two of us in Italy, earning eight hundred euros a month… You'll wonder what you were ever so worried about!"

Natalia started up the engine and quickly drove away.

Chapter Four

Natalia sat in her family's weather-beaten farmhouse with her nephew Valery in her lap. She held a brush in one hand and ran it through the child's hair, his head gently bobbing with each stroke. Nearby, Olga held squirming Tatiana while Constantine played with wooden cars on the floor, wheezing noises coming from his labored breathing.

"It must be so strange for you here," said Natalia. "Without Leon around."

Olga appeared bewildered by the comment but said nothing in return.

"I mean, living with a family that's not your own..."

"You'd prefer that I left?!" Olga replied.

"No, that's not it at all."

"And take the children with me? You think I should go back to my parents' place?"

"No, no! I'm sorry, I just... I guess what I'm trying to say is that life is not so bad here, really, is it?"

Olga tilted her head sideways slightly as she studied Natalia's face. "Are we really talking about me?"

"Why do you say that?"

"I always knew you had a little of your brother in you. That wild streak. It comes from your mother, you know."

"I can't see what that has to do with anything."

"You're leaving us. Aren't you? It doesn't surprise me. I've been expecting it."

"I haven't made any decisions."

"Did you hope I'd talk you out of it? That I'd tell you to stay here on the farm where you belong? If you really wanted that advice, you'd have gone to someone else."

"I wasn't looking for advice."

"Then why bring it up at all?"

"I didn't realize that I had. But now that we're talking about it, think of the money I could send back to you and the children if I did go," Natalia tried to justify herself. "It could make such a difference."

"Don't go for us. Go for yourself, if that's what you want. Go because the life you deserve is out there somewhere. We'll get along without you."

Before Natalia could say any more, the front door opened and Rita bounded in. "What's going on in here?"

"Your sister was just telling me that she's leaving us," Olga said.

Natalia's pulse quickened. There it was, out in the open.

"Leaving us?" said Rita. "What are you talking about? Where are you going?"

"Maybe to Italy. But only for a little while," said Natalia.

"Italy!" Rita replied. "I want to go to Italy!"

"It's ok, don't be so upset," said Natalia.

"How come you get to go to Italy? It's not fair! I'll have to do twice the work!"

Natalia rose to her feet and took Rita by the shoulders before leaning forward to kiss her on the forehead. "You I will miss the most." She wrapped her arms around her sister and embraced her tightly. The decision was made. Natalia was leaving after all.

Sitting on a small wooden bench in front of the barn, Natalia sent a quick text to her boyfriend Vitaly as daylight faded from the sky. *Can you talk?* A moment later, her phone rang. "Hi, Vitaly," she answered.

"What's up?"

"Not much, how are you?"

"Bored. God, it's so damn boring here. I can't wait until it's over already."

"Just a few more months."

"Yeah. A few more months."

"It's not so exciting around here, either."

"At least there's no sergeant breathing down your neck all the time."

"Is it that bad?"

"I'll be surprised if I don't strangle that son-of-a-bitch before I'm done."

"Don't do anything foolish."

Vitaly's desperation was evident in the ensuing pause. "I think of you, waiting for me. That's what gets me through."

Now it was Natalia's turn to feel pressured. "I'm glad, Vitaly. I am."

"Why does that sound so unconvincing?"

"There's something I have to tell you. I'm going away for a while."

"Going where? For how long?!"

"Sonia and I are going to Italy. We found some jobs there."

"Damn it, Natalia, two more months and I'll be back home! You can't do this to me!"

"I'm sorry, Vitaly. Maybe you can come to visit me."

"You know I can't do that, Natalia. I have the farm to think about!"

"Really, Vitaly, I'm sorry. I'll be back before you know it, I promise. It's only temporary."

"Can't we talk about this later? Don't make any hasty decisions. You need to think this through."

"I already have. I'm going."

"Don't do this, Natalia!"

"I'm sorry. I'll talk to you soon." Only when Natalia hung up did she realize that she hadn't said those three magic words. Maybe it wasn't too late. *I love you,* she texted. As the first stars began blinking on high above, she sat and waited for a response. None came.

Chapter Five

With the Nicolaev family gathered outside to bid Natalia farewell, Ivanka struggled to keep up her stoic appearance. "Let go of her!" she scolded the two boys, who clung to Natalia's legs. "Go on!" She shooed them away and moved in to give her daughter a bear hug.

"Careful momma, you'll squeeze the wind out of me!" Natalia tried to laugh.

"Any girl of mine is strong enough for a hug." Ivanka squeezed even harder before releasing her daughter to take a good last look. "You be careful out there, and don't forget us!"

"After that hug? Never." Natalia did her best to keep the mood light. She wasn't used to goodbyes. Not like this. The last time she left, she'd run off without a word, sneaking away on a cold winter morning to Tiraspol, the capital of this forlorn breakaway republic of Transnistria. After one week hunting for her brother Leon, she'd finally found him living in an abandoned building, no water no power. She'd thought she would bring him home with her, but Leon had other ideas, and so Natalia came back to Drosti on her own, devastated by her failure. This time she fought a different swirl of emotions as she prepared to leave once more, from anxiety about the journey ahead to elation that she was actually going through with it. From joy at the adventures awaiting her to sorrow at leaving familiarity behind.

"You'd better write to us," said Olga. "Only don't make it sound too good or I might come and join you."

"As long as you bring the kids along," Natalia smiled at her nephews.

"We'd better get going or you'll miss the train," said Victor.

"Can I ride with you to the station, papa?" Rita asked and their father nodded his assent.

After a few last kisses for the children, Natalia climbed into the car and pulled the front passenger door shut behind her. With her sister in the back and father behind the wheel, they moved off down the dirt track. Natalia waved one hand out the window all the way up and over the rise until they were out of sight. On toward the village, Natalia was struck by an unexpected exuberance. She was off to see the world! For the first time in her life, it truly was wide open.

"I'll bet you'll meet some cute Italian boy and never come back," said Rita.

"Maybe I'll bring him back with me."

"Ha!" Rita laughed out loud.

"What's so funny?" her father asked.

"What Italian boy would want to live here?" Rita continued. "I just hope he has a cute brother!"

"You know I already have Vitaly." As soon as Natalia spoke the words, she wondered if they were true.

At the train station, Victor carried Natalia's suitcase to the platform where Sonia stood waiting beside her mother and Svetlana. "There she is!" Sonia waved happily.

"All ready for your big adventure?" Svetlana asked with a quick smile.

"As ready as I will be," Natalia replied.

"I have your passport here." Svetlana pulled the brand new document from her bag and handed it over; burgundy on the cover, with the Moldovan coat of arms embossed in the center. Natalia opened the first page to see her photo staring back. "Look at this papa," she said, "My own passport!"

Victor merely grunted, but she could tell he was impressed. His daughter was the first in his family ever to have one.

"Let me see, let me see!" Rita snatched the passport from Natalia's hand. "Wow! I want one of these."

"No!" said Victor. "One daughter running off is enough."

"Aw, it's just not fair…"

Natalia took the passport back as a relic of a train rolled into the station, boxy green engine belching black smoke into the sky. The ancient, rusting cars slowed to a stop beside the platform and Natalia kissed her father on the cheek before holding Rita in a long, last embrace. By the time she let go, Sonia and Svetlana were already climbing on board.

"Come on, it won't stop long!" said Sonia.

Natalia followed them up the carriage steps, turning back to take the suitcase from her father's outstretched hands. His cheeks flushed red. "Be careful out there," he said, though the true depth of feeling was conveyed by his eyes. Natalia paused where she was, touched by his uncharacteristic show of emotion. Her father, who had always been larger than life, suddenly seemed so very small.

"Don't worry about me," said Natalia. "We're a family of strong women, remember?"

Victor allowed himself to smile. "How could I forget?"

"Goodbye, father." Natalia moved on into the carriage, hoisting her bag onto a luggage rack before finding a seat by the window.

"We're off!" said Sonia from the seat just across. "I can hardly believe this day has finally come."

As the train eased forward, Natalia kept her eyes on her father, with hands pushed deeply into his pockets. Beside him, her sister waved enthusiastically with one hand while holding her phone in the other to film the scene for posterity. "So long, don't forget us!"

Soon they were out of sight as the train picked up speed until it was sailing along the iron tracks, a rhythmic *click-clack, click-clack, click-clack* keeping time. Tomorrow they would see Odessa and the Black Sea. Natalia leaned her head against the window as the little village of Drosti faded into the distance.

Chapter Six

Climbing off the train, Natalia was assaulted by the noise, hustle and bustle of Odessa's main railway station. She'd never seen so many people in one place, and all of them intent on where they were going, hurrying along with grim determination. It made Tiraspol seem quaint by comparison. Natalia gazed upwards to marvel at the glass panels arcing high above their heads, held in place by rusting iron beams.

"Stay close, I don't want to lose you." Svetlana ushered the girls down the platform and out the main door to the street.

"Taxi? Do you need a taxi?" Eager cab drivers converged on the new arrivals.

"My car is right here!" One man waved an arm to show them a beat-up gypsy cab parked at the curb. Svetlana ignored him, continuing on instead to the official taxi stand where she said a few quick words to a driver with central Asian features and dark, straight hair. He loaded their bags into his trunk. Sonia and Natalia settled into the back seat. Svetlana took the front and they were off, Natalia watching out the window as they moved through the city in all of its chaos and glory; giant buildings and crowded sidewalks, roadways throbbing with traffic. Mostly she looked at the people, as though she might somehow divine what was going through their minds. What was it like to live in such a city? Her heart raced at the prospect.

When they arrived at the ferry dock, Svetlana opened her purse and pulled out enough money to pay the cab fare. Even such a simple transaction was enough to mystify Natalia. Did the man expect exact change? Or should there be a tip? Should Natalia contribute? All she knew for sure was that these nuances of big city life were wholly beyond her. When they'd retrieved their bags at the curb, Svetlana led the girls into the terminal building. Through windows on the far side, Natalia saw a massive white ship tied up to the dock. Giant blue letters adorned the hull: UKR FERRY. Smoke streamed upwards from a single blue smokestack. "Yuzhnaya Palmyra," Natalia mouthed the name written across the bow as she took a few steps closer to get a better look.

"Natalia!" Svetlana chided her. "Don't wander off!"

"I'm sorry." Natalia felt like a scolded child.

"We need to meet the others," Svetlana added.

"Others? What others?"

"There they are!" Svetlana waved across the hall to three girls about Natalia's age who stood together under a large round clock, their own luggage resting on the floor nearby. Svetlana moved across to greet them, planting kisses on their cheeks in turn. "Hello, hello! I hope you weren't waiting long!"

Natalia looked from girl to girl, sizing them up in turn. One was larger than the others and tall, with hair cascading down her shoulders in long blonde curls. She had full features and a resigned look on her face, as though she'd prefer to be anywhere else. Another was small and mousy, with dark hair and a thin nose. She seemed nervous, with wide eyes darting back and forth. The third girl was the prettiest of them all, with gleaming brown hair and makeup carefully applied to her cheeks, her lips, her eyes. She wore a camel's hair jacket over jeans with brown leather shoes. Her head was tilted back, causing her to look down on everything around her with a hint of disdain. It was enough to give Natalia a quick pulse of insecurity. "Who are they?" she whispered, but Sonia simply furrowed her brow and shrugged.

"Come, meet your traveling companions!" Svetlana motioned them over.

"How many waitresses does this restaurant need?" Natalia asked Svetlana as they approached.

"Victoria and Maria are to work as nannies, in Greece. And Helena won a modeling contest. She's headed to Rome." Svetlana placed a hand on the pretty girl's shoulder. "I'm sorry. Perhaps I should have mentioned that they would be joining us."

"It does seem odd," said Natalia in return.

"No, not odd at all. I work for a private employment agency, searching for bright, honest, hard-working girls like yourselves. You didn't think I was taking you to Italy merely out of the goodness of my heart, did you?" Svetlana raised her eyebrows. "Just because I get a little something out of it doesn't mean anything has changed."

Natalia felt a swell of apprehension. It had been there all along, lurking in the background, ever since she'd first met Svetlana. Something about the woman's manner had always seemed insincere, as though she were sharing only just enough information to keep the girls in line and no more. This latest revelation certainly didn't inspire further confidence. Why hadn't she bothered to mention it before? And what else was she keeping from them?

"It's fine, Natalia, really." Sonia tried to play the diplomat. Of course, she wanted to believe what she was told. Her fantasy depended on it. Natalia wasn't so sure. She would keep an eye on Svetlana, whose saccharine smile didn't reassure her. At the very least, this woman wasn't here to do the girls any favors. That much was clear. Whatever the payoff, Svetlana was in this entirely for herself.

"I'm Maria." The mousy-looking girl gave them a quick wave.

"Victoria," said the tall one.

Natalia turned to the pretty one. "And you're Helena," she said.

"That's right." Helena gave a nod.

"Come girls, we'll have plenty of time to talk on board the ship," said Svetlana.

The five girls crowded into a windowless interior cabin, eying three sets of bunks. "This one's mine." Helena heaved her suitcase onto one of the bottom berths. The other girls followed suit, choosing beds of their own while Svetlana watched from the doorway.

"How long will the trip take?" asked Maria.

"Twenty-four hours. We arrive in Istanbul in the afternoon at 14:30 and then change to another ship for the next leg. I'm going to get some rest. If you girls need anything at all, please give a knock on my door. I'm right across the hall."

When Svetlana was gone, the girls stared at each other blankly, unsure what to do next. "Why don't we go check out the ship?" said Victoria.

"That's a good idea," said Sonia. "Maybe we'll find some boys to talk to."

"Oh no, that's the last thing I need," said Helena with contempt.

"What's wrong, you have a boyfriend back home?" asked Sonia.

"A *fiancé*," Helena corrected her.

"Lucky you," said Sonia. "Is he handsome?"

"Of course he is."

The girls left the cabin and made their way down the passageway, through a set of double doors and into the nearest lounge. Women cradled crying babies and the smell of unwashed bodies filled the air. A middle-aged man with uncombed dark hair and dirty clothing peered at the five attractive young women. Natalia met his gaze, staring him down until he turned and hobbled off, muttering to himself in a foreign tongue.

"It was nice of Svetlana to book a cabin for us," said Maria. "I'd hate to have to sleep out here."

"She's a good woman," Victoria agreed. "She reminds me of my grandmother."

The girls found space on a set of couches along one wall. Helena pulled out her phone. "They better have wifi on this tub, that's all I have to say." She scrolled through her settings.

"I'll bet you have to pay." Victoria took out her own.

"Damn it!" Helena's response confirmed their suspicions. "Ten euros, are you kidding me?"

"I think we'll survive without it," said Natalia.

Maybe we can get Svetlana to pay." Helena put her phone down. "

"Doesn't your fiancé worry about you going abroad?" Sonia asked Helena. "Maybe you will find another man, with more money."

Helena merely shrugged. The idea didn't seem to faze her, as though she'd already considered it herself.

"I hope *I* do," Sonia added wistfully. "A rich Italian man."

"Have any of you been abroad before?" Victoria asked.

"Not yet," said Helena. "But it won't be the last time."

Natalia's attention turned toward two small children playing near their mother. A boy taunted his younger sister, waving a plastic straw in front of her face. Unperturbed, the girl gamely reached for it each time, smiling as her brother pulled it just out of reach. After the fourth time, she suddenly burst into tears, mouth open wide as she wailed at full volume. This elicited a smile from the brother and a scolding from the mother, who snatched the straw away. Reminded of her niece and nephews, Natalia felt a pang of emotion.

"Kids can be such brats." Sonia eyed the little boy, still looking smug over the commotion he'd caused.

"Some of them," said Natalia.

"I suppose you'll have your own slew of children. You and Vitaly with a house full of mouths to feed?"

"You want kids, too, Sonia. I know you do."

"Someday," Sonia acknowledged quietly. "When I'm ready. I just hope they'll behave themselves."

"Good luck," Natalia laughed. "Karma can be cruel."

"What?! I wasn't a bad kid!" Sonia protested. "Maybe a little precocious…"

The ship's horn sounded as the ferry pulled away from the dock. "I want to see the view." Natalia stood but none of the others made a move, so she walked on her own through a doorway and out onto the deck, leaning against the rail with the wind in her face. In the bow, she saw a small group of seamen pulling in the lines and coiling them carefully at their feet. The ship picked up speed as it moved into the harbor. Across the water, a row of giant metal cranes rose like some fantastic creatures from another world. To Natalia this *was* another world, and yet she knew it was only the beginning. Despite her misgivings, she couldn't help but be excited.

"It is beautiful, isn't it?" came Sonia's voice as she joined Natalia at the rail.

Natalia nodded, watching the afternoon sun shimmer off the water.

"Can you believe we've actually done it?" Sonia broke into a giddy smile. "We've really done it! We finally got out of that little shit-hole of a village, at last!"

"It is hard to believe. I feel like my whole life is ahead of me."

"Don't forget, I'm the one that dragged you out of there."

"I know you did."

"The rest of those people can go to hell as far as I'm concerned." There was a bitterness in Sonia's voice, her cheeks showing a hint of scarlet. "They're small-minded people in a small-minded place. I hope I never go back!"

"You can't mean that."

"Oh, I mean it! I never want to see any of those people ever again."

"What about your mother?" Natalia asked.

Sonia grasped the rail so tightly that the knuckles on both hands turned white. She stared straight ahead. "My mother can come see me. In Italy."

Natalia sighed. "I hope you don't expect *me* to stay there forever."

"You can do what you want."

They stood side-by-side looking over the water, Natalia confused and Sonia quietly fuming. "You got what you always wanted," Natalia said. "Maybe you should relax and enjoy it."

"Yes. I got what I wanted." Sonia dropped her head, a single tear rolling down the side of her cheek.

"What is it?" Natalia asked. "What aren't you telling me?" The first tear was followed by another, and then another until Sonia was heaving giant sobs, wracked by spasms of grief. Natalia tried to make sense of this sudden outburst but couldn't manage. Sonia's dreams were finally being realized. Was it simply too much for her? Natalia placed a hand on Sonia's back. "Don't worry, everything is going to be wonderful, just like you always imagined."

Sonia wiped one cheek, struggling to compose herself. "You think I'm just being emotional, is that it?"

"Is there something else?"

"I'm going to have a baby, Natalia."

The words hung in the air. Natalia stood up straight, mouth open wide, feeling as though the wind had been knocked clean out of her. "When? How???"

Sonia's cheeks turned a darker shade of red. "I don't want to talk about that. I'm sorry."

"Ivan? Is it Ivan's baby?"

"Natalia, don't ask me that question again!" Sonia was stern. "It's going to be my little Italian baby, that's all you need to know! That's all anyone needs to know!"

"But, you'll be alone. Who is going to help you?"

"You're my family, Natalia, as much as anyone. I'll have you."

Natalia was quiet, unwilling to let on how frightened this was. In her mind, she'd only committed to three months in Italy. Stay for the summer and then reevaluate in the fall. Now Sonia was expecting her to stay for the term of this child, and then to help raise it besides? This was a level of responsibility Natalia didn't think she could handle, but what was the alternative? Abandon Sonia in her time of need? Natalia stared out across the sea, trying to resign herself to whatever future lay before them. "It's going to be all right," she said, and then repeated the words, speaking to herself as much as to Sonia. "It's going to be all right."

Chapter Seven

The waters were crowded with rusted freighters and aging oil tankers moving in either direction through a narrow straight. Natalia couldn't keep from staring out the window. The shore looked so close it seemed that she could nearly reach out and touch it. Excusing herself from the others, she made her way up a set of stairs and forward, to a deck above the bridge. From here she could see everything.

"The Bosporus," said a man nearby. He was stocky, in a black leather coat with a large, rutted face that showed the marks of age and hard living. He eyed her curiously, cigarette between two fingers. "Asia on one side and Europe on the other," he gestured.

"I see." Natalia gave him a quick once-over before turning away.

"Not much farther," added the man. "Forty minutes perhaps."

Natalia nodded in response, eyeing the olive-green, brush-covered hills, so different from the rolling fields of Drosti. An ancient stone fortress sat crumbling atop a hill on the Asian side, with a tiny seaside village tucked below. Red umbrellas provided shade for outdoor cafes along the water. Green, blue and yellow fishing boats bobbed at anchor before them. Atop a ridge on the European side, an enormous flag fluttered in the breeze; deep red with a single star and crescent moon. Natalia felt so very far from home.

At one of the cafes, she spotted a young waitress in a black blouse and skirt, carrying coffee on a tray. "Soon, that will be me," Natalia said to herself, watching as the waitress placed the coffee on the table of a single, lounging customer. She felt a guarded sense of optimism, though she still couldn't fully shake her apprehensions. It was no wonder that Sonia seemed so desperate to get out of Drosti in the last few weeks. People would have started talking as soon as the baby began to show. Who was the father? Everyone would want to know that. Natalia wanted to know. Was it Ivan after all? They'd stopped seeing each other more than six months earlier, but who else was there? Natalia sighed. When Sonia was ready to talk about it, she'd talk about it. Until then there was no use in speculating.

"This bridge connects two continents." The man in black moved closer, pointing to a span strung across the water just ahead.

Natalia glanced at him warily and then looked up to the bridge, where a stream of cars and trucks flowed across above them. Along the shoreline she saw enormous homes, unlike any she could have imagined before, each one several stories high with manicured gardens and their own private docks in front.

"Must be nice, huh?" The man followed her eyes.

"I don't know. With all that room, I think I'd be lonely."

"Your first time in Istanbul?" he asked.

"My first time anywhere, really."

"If you'd like, I could show you around…"

"Oh, no, I am not staying. We'll catch another boat from here."

"That is a pity," said the man.

"Yes, it looks like a wonderful place."

"Dolmabahce Palace." The man pointed to a long, beautifully ornate building set along the water on the port side. "The sultans lived there. The Ottomans, you know. When this was an empire."

Natalia nodded, unable to hide her fascination. She pulled out her phone and snapped a quick photo. As they came upon the heart of the city she was struck by the sheer size of it, with buildings packed so tightly together and massive domed mosques rising from every hill and knoll, their pointed minarets reaching skyward.

"There you are!" Sonia made her way up the stairway and across the deck to Natalia's side. "Svetlana wants us to get ready!"

Natalia recoiled, struck by Sonia's bright red lips and the pink rouge on her cheeks. "Why did you put that makeup on?"

"She wants us to make a good impression."

"On whom?" Natalia asked in confusion.

"I don't know. Immigration, maybe."

Natalia squinted and pursed her own lips, trying to find some logic in this.

"Come on, we don't have much time," said Sonia. "The other girls are almost ready to go."

Natalia took one last look forward. She saw the deckhands in the bow readying the lines for arrival. "All right, I'm coming." She turned to the man beside her. "It was nice talking to you."

"My pleasure, enjoy your travels," he replied with a nod.

Natalia followed Sonia across the deck and down the stairs, on toward the next leg of their journey.

In the immigration hall, Svetlana guided the girls along like a mother duckling tending her chicks. The entire flock attracted plenty of attention from the other passengers, though the girls hardly noticed, so intent were they on trying to orient themselves in this unfamiliar environment. Svetlana herded them to the end of a long line leading to one in a row of glass-enclosed booths with the words Pasaport Kontrol printed across the top in large blue letters. Inside each booth was an immigration officer, scrutinizing the passengers' documents in turn.

Svetlana handed out the passports to each girl. On instinct, they gingerly flipped through the pages to look again at their photos. At the front of the line, an officer waved Svetlana forward with one hand. She brought the whole group to the desk in a pack, but the officer shook his head. "Her seferinde bir," he said. Ignoring him, Svetlana produced her own passport and slid it through a hole in the glass. Natalia watched as the officer picked it up and looked inside, carefully palming a wad of hidden bills. He raised his head again and looked in both directions before stamping the passport and sliding it back.

"Come girls, passports, passports!" Svetlana cheerfully picked hers up.

One by one the girls slid their own passports under the glass and the agent stamped them, hardly bothering to look at all. Finally, with a flick of the wrist, he motioned for the girls to go on through. They hustled past a pair of idle Turkish policemen, machine guns slung from their shoulders as they eyed the girls with nonchalance. Out on the street, pedestrians and peddlers jostled for position. Taxi drivers accosted them once again from all sides, shouting in Turkish, English and Russian.

"Give me your passports girls!" Svetlana as they stood on the sidewalk in the midst of the maelstrom. One by one the girls handed over their documents.

"I'd rather hold my own," said Natalia.

"I'm sorry, but I prefer to look after them, to be on the safe side," Svetlana countered. "I wouldn't want you to lose it." Natalia hesitantly placed her passport in the older woman's hand, even while she wondered why there'd been a payoff. Was something wrong? Again Natalia felt manipulated, but she had little time to ponder the reason.

"Follow me!" Svetlana commanded, wheeling her suitcase down the street with the girls in tow. When they came to a large black van by the curb, Svetlana halted. Inside sat two burly men, one in a suit and the other a black leather jacket. One climbed out and opened the side door.

"Where are we going?" asked Maria.

"The next leg of our excursion," said Svetlana. "Go ahead, climb in. Find room for the bags wherever you can."

The girls did as they were told, including an increasingly anxious Natalia. Any feeling of control was quickly evaporating.

"What about the other boat?" Sonia asked Natalia under her breath. The van door slammed shut and a moment later they were off; five naive girls staring out the windows at a strange, exotic land.

The van crossed a bridge and continued up a winding hill, past a mosque and then down a busy, crowded street. Groups of dark-haired men gathered in front of small markets, bakeries and kabob shops. Taxis parked in clusters at street corners, their drivers chatting lazily. Women in headscarves and dark robes walked in pairs, shopping bags in hand.

"Where are we going?" Sonia whispered.

"I don't know," Natalia answered, trying to calm her own fears as well. The van turned down an alley and stopped behind two parked cars; one a non-descript sedan and the other a sleek black Mercedes. Two more men in suits climbed out of each car. The driver of the Mercedes stroked a trim black beard as he peered through the window at the girls. His hair was short and dark. His suit seemed better tailored than the others. On his wrist was an expensive-looking watch. When their eyes met, Natalia tried to get a read on the man. Where she might have expected malevolence, she saw instead a dull boredom. He blinked twice and moved on.

"Wait here a moment," said Svetlana. Any sign of her previously pleasant demeanor was gone. She climbed from the van and slammed the door closed before walking off a short distance with the bearded man. The girls watched them have a brief discussion before the man pulled out a thick stack of bills and placed them in Svetlana's hand. She quickly counted the money before stuffing it into a pocket. Svetlana struggled to stifle the creeping lines of a wicked smile as she handed over the girls' five passports. The man nodded his head as if vaguely satisfied with the transaction. Svetlana walked to the sedan and climbed into the passenger seat as one of the other men climbed in on the driver's side. She held her chin high, jaw clenched tight as the man started the car and pulled away.

"Where is she going? What's happening?" The panic in Sonia's voice betrayed her. She knew. They all knew.

"We'll stick together," Natalia said. "We'll get out of this. I promise you. We have each other." She fought to keep the terror from overtaking her. Another of the men climbed inside the van and the driver started the engine and pulled out of the alley.

"Where are we going?!" Helena began to scream. "I demand that you tell me where you are taking us! Stop this van right now!"

"Keep your mouth shut!" said the man in the front passenger seat.

"That's it, I'm calling the police!" Helena took out her phone from a small purse. She'd just begun to dial when the man reached back and gripped her wrist. "Ow, you're hurting me!"

The man pried the device from her hand. "The rest of you, pass me your phones, now!"

"I don't have a phone," said Victoria.

"Just do as he says," Natalia replied.

One by one, the girls handed their phones forward to the man, who stacked them up and then slid them into the glove compartment. Maria began to shake uncontrollably, eyes darting to and fro, fingers digging into the vinyl seat.

"What about Italy?" said Sonia.

"There is no Italy," Natalia answered.

"What has she done to us?"

"She's sold us," said Natalia, a wave of nausea passing over her.

Chapter Eight

The van pulled onto another narrow side street between hulking concrete apartment buildings. The Mercedes followed closely behind as they continued half a block and then came to a stop. The men in the car hopped out and quickly approached the van. One of them, burly with a shaved head and tattoos on his neck, opened the van door and shouted at the girls in Russian. "Out!" he yelled. The girls flinched but stayed where they were.

"Let's go," said the man with the beard, waving an arm to coax them along. "Bring your luggage!" Natalia climbed out first with her suitcase in hand, looking in both directions for a way to flee. They were boxed in on all sides, and even if she did manage to escape, she couldn't run off and leave Sonia behind. A metal door covered in scrawls of graffiti swung open to reveal yet another man; this one skinny and pale with circles under his eyes and a cigarette dangling lazily from his lips. Natalia looked up at the building's exterior. High above, five women in skimpy negligees crowded onto a top-floor balcony, gazing down with mild curiosity. Natalia's worst nightmare was coming true, and there seemed to be nothing she could do to stop it.

"Where are we going?" Next out, Victoria was still not quite clear on the concept of what was happening to them.

"Move it! Inside!" The burly man raised a hand as if to strike her. Victoria cringed and pressed forward against Natalia, who went on through the door with the rest of the girls trailing behind. The pale, thin man led them up a dark and decrepit staircase, with paint peeling from the railings and the walls. The unmistakable odor of urine hung in the dank, stale air. Up and around they went, lugging their heavy bags until they reached another solid steel door on the fifth floor. Beside it was a chair, with a stack of old magazines on the floor beside it. The man reached into his pocket and pulled out a rattling cluster of keys, fiddled until he found the correct one and slid it into one of several locks, turning it to the right. When the door swung open, he motioned the girls on through.

With the other men standing behind them on the stairs, Natalia knew there was no alternative. Not yet. She would fight this, there was no question, but she'd have to pick the time, when the odds weren't stacked so brutally against them. Natalia moved on into a dimly-lit lounge with peeling gilt wallpaper. Plush green couches were arranged along two walls. Standing to their left was a middle-aged woman, arms crossed. She had long dark hair framing a stark and sallow face. She may have been pretty once, Natalia thought, but her beauty was gone, replaced by creased skin and hollow eyes. She wore a black dress cut below the knees with black flats on her feet. The woman examined each girl in turn as they entered the room, followed closely by the small crowd of thugs. From the balcony, the other women came inside as well, to get a better look at the fresh meat. The pale key-master shut the door from the outside and Natalia heard the ominous sound of the key turning in the bolt as he locked them all in.

"Sit!" the sallow-faced woman commanded. All but Helena obeyed, dropping their suitcases and finding seats on the green couches.

Showing no sign of apprehension, Helena took on an air of provocation. "I demand to be released from this place!" she shouted. "How dare you bring us here?! I have a ship to catch!"

"Sit!" The madam pointed to a couch.

"I will not!" Helena countered. Before she could speak again, the shaved-headed thug flew across the room and shoved her violently off her feet, sending her sprawling, half on the couch and half on the floor. It took Helena a moment to regain her composure and jump back up. This time the man punched her in the stomach before shoving her straight to the ground where she lay, choking for air. Natalia grasped Sonia's hand, clutching it tightly in her own.

"If she doesn't climb onto that couch in five seconds, kick her," the woman said. "Anywhere but the face. Such a pretty face."

The man wound up to kick as Helena tried desperately to pull herself onto the couch. She dragged herself off the floor, still wheezing as she lay beside the horrified Maria.

"I am Ludmilla. You will do exactly as I say. If you cooperate, you will find our work conditions bearable. If you do not cooperate…" The woman nodded toward Helena. "This will be as hard for you as you make it."

"What work?" said Victoria.

"What work?" the woman repeated, as if in disbelief. "I think you know why you're here."

"No!" gasped Maria, shaking her head.

"No?" the woman raised her eyebrows. "This is not a question. You will work until you have paid your debts. After that it is up to you if you want to remain."

"What debts?" Natalia asked. "We have no debts."

"Each of you owes us five thousand euros," the woman answered.

"Five thousand…!" said Sonia.

"That was your purchase price, plus the cost of transportation and documentation. You will also owe us rent and the cost of your food. Some girls are able to pay off their debt in as little as four or five months."

"I am no prostitute!" Helena growled from her place on the couch. "I owe you nothing!"

Ludmilla shrugged. "Show her the view," she said to the thugs, who set upon her, dragging her, half by her hair and half by an arm, through an open doorway and onto the balcony. They flung her over the rail, grasping her legs as she dangled five stories above the sidewalk below. From her spot on the couch, Natalia remained frozen, unable to think, unable to move.

"Wait!" Ludmilla shouted. "That one is too pretty. Take this little one!" She motioned toward Maria, whose eyes grew wider as the men pulled Helena off the balcony and dropped her like a rag doll. They were on Maria next, hauling her past Helena and then dangling her over the abyss. Too frightened to scream, Maria made only faint, squeaking noises as they jostled her up and down.

"You wouldn't!" screamed Helena from her spot on the floor.

"Oh, we most certainly would," Ludmilla sneered. "And it wouldn't be the first time."

The man with the beard had only watched the proceedings until this point but now moved calmly across the room until he stood over Helena. "If they drop her, you will owe me 10,000 euros." The man grabbed her by an arm and dragged her across the floor through another door, slamming it shut behind them. The others heard screams, and then a series of blows. Ludmilla nodded to the men on the balcony, who pulled Maria back over to the floor and let her go. She scampered to the couch and rolled up into a ball.

"I take it we won't have any problems with the rest of you," said Ludmilla. From inside the other room, the banging noises continued, with screams replaced by an occasional whimper. Natalia's eyes darted back and forth as she tried desperately to process the reality of the situation. The door to the next room swung open and the bearded man reappeared first, zipping up his fly as he glared from one girl to the next in defiance. When his eyes met Natalia's he paused. She was the only one who didn't look away. They locked onto one another for several long seconds. Where there'd been boredom in those eyes before, now she saw… ecstasy? Natalia wasn't sure exactly. The man's entire state of consciousness had shifted, as though inflicting terror was the drug that he thrived on. It was only Natalia's refusal to look away that seemed to diminish his bliss, though he quickly shook it off. He turned to his henchmen. "Come, we go!" He spoke in Russian, but with an accent that Natalia couldn't place. It was not his first language. Wherever he was from, this was the man who held the key to their freedom. With his beard and his accent and his gratification in the suffering of those less powerful than himself… he was the head of this distorted depravity in which Natalia and the others found themselves. This man whose wild, unfocused eyes gave away his evil nature. He was dangerous and unpredictable, and that was ultimately where his power lay. Natalia remembered Multinovic, hiding in her village from some unspeakable past. Multinovic had the reputation for evil, but Natalia never really saw it in him. Not like she saw now. With this one it was plain as day.

The man moved quickly to the front door and wrapped three times with his knuckles. The bolt slid in the lock and the door opened, the pale key master standing just outside. The rest of the men followed one by one into the hall before the door was closed and locked behind them once again. Natalia and Victoria moved quickly to Helena as she crawled back into the lounge, hair in her face, her skirt pulled down to her ankles.

"Tanya, show these girls around and get them ready to work!" Ludmilla moved down a hallway, leaving the newcomers and the veterans to scrutinize one another.

"Welcome to hell." The girl who spoke was tall, with long dark hair and olive skin.

Another girl stepped forward, thin with reddish-brown hair and freckles, wearing a lacy black negligee. There was an air of fatalism in the way she held herself, with her head tilted back slightly. "You'll get used to it."

"What if we don't want to get used to it?" Natalia placed one calming hand on Helena's back.

"You have to. It's your only option. Either that or you can jump." The girl nodded toward the balcony.

Natalia looked to the others in silence. How could this have happened? She'd thought she was being so careful. But then she'd never really trusted Svetlana. There was always that feeling, deep in Natalia's gut. The sense that something wasn't right. Natalia had allowed her instincts to be overruled. She'd believed Svetlana because she wanted to believe. For Sonia's sake, and for her own. The fantasy was simply too strong a lure. Natalia always thought that this kind of thing only happened to promiscuous girls, or naïve ones, but maybe Natalia was more naïve than she'd thought. "Let's get her up," she said to Victoria. They helped Helena to her feet, pulled her skirt to her waist and then eased her onto one of the couches.

"There must be some way out!" Sonia had the desperate demeanor of a caged animal as she paced the room, moving to the front door to try the knob.

"There's an armed guard at all times," said the dark-haired girl.

"That skinny man with the cigarette?" Natalia scoffed. "Surely we can handle him!"

"No, there are others. Always others. You'll learn. It's best not to cross them."

"But how can they get away with this?" Victoria seethed. "What about the police?"

"Forget the police. Unless they're customers, we don't see the police," said the redhead. "Come on, I'll show you around. We're open for business all day, so you better be ready."

"I won't do it." Helena slumped on the couch in a daze. She struggled to maintain her defiance but the fire had left her and she hung her head, eyes glazed, disbelieving.

"What don't you understand?" the redhead scoffed. "You have two choices. You either do it or they kill you. Believe me, they *will* kill you."

Sonia looked at Natalia in sorrow. "I'm sorry… I'm so sorry…"

"This is not your fault," Natalia replied. "Don't say it. Don't think it."

An intercom buzzed and the veterans perked up. Ludmilla reappeared and pressed a button before speaking into a box on the wall. "Fifth floor, come on up."

"Time to work," said the redhead. "My name is Tanya. You new girls bring your things and come with me." She led them down a hallway and into the back, past a row of rooms where she stopped to swing one of the doors open. Inside was a double bed, a nightstand and a dresser. "You'll each be given a room of your own. You will work and sleep in these rooms. Condoms are in the nightstand, but if your customer doesn't want you to use them, you don't use them. Understand?"

"You can't mean that!" said Natalia.

"Those are the rules. I didn't make them."

Natalia was struck by the sense that she would die here. It was she who would be splayed out on the concrete five stories down, neck snapped in two. If they didn't throw her, she might actually jump. If those were her choices, to let them subjugate her body and her soul or to die, she'd almost rather die. But Natalia had more fight in her than that. There must be a third way, she told herself.

There must be some way out. Natalia understood that she couldn't follow Helena's lead. A test of wills would get her nowhere. Instead, she'd go along until she found a proper means of escape for her and Sonia both, if only they could survive that long.

Continuing down the hallway, Tanya motioned to the row of doors. "These rooms are open. Take your pick. That last door on the left is the bathroom. We share it so keep it clean! The clients' bathroom is by the front door. You are never allowed to use the clients' bathroom, understand?" The girls stared back at Tanya with blank expressions, struggling to grasp how she could make it all sound so normal. Just another day of "work." Simply the way of the world. "I'll take that as a yes. You can leave your bags here for now." Tanya turned left down another hall and led them into a store room. An open bureau was full of underwear and skimpy satin negligees. "Pick out a few things to wear." She stood to one side, but the girls remained motionless where they stood. "Ok, fine," Tanya's tone betrayed her annoyance. She rummaged through the undergarments on her own, picking out one here and another there before handing them over to the girls. When everyone had an item or two, the tour continued, back into the hall and then through a door at the end which opened into a kitchen area with a large dining table in the middle. In one corner sat an older woman with frizzy dark hair and a square head. She wore a polyester print dress and looked up briefly from a dated Russian magazine.

"This is Galina," said Tanya. "She cooks our meals. Three a day, beginning with breakfast at 7 a.m." In the front room, they heard a doorbell ring, followed by the squeak of the hinges as the front door swung open. "Come along, it is time to change and be ready to work."

Chapter Nine

Natalia sat on a couch beside the others wearing nothing but a green silk slip. She'd had sex with exactly one man in her life. The man she planned to marry. It was a shocking realization that her own body, her flesh itself, was a commodity that could be bought and sold. This was something that other women did. Not Natalia Nicolaeva. Not this quiet farm girl. She looked at her leg peeking out from under the shimmering undergarment. This leg of hers that was for sale. This leg which she'd always assumed was her own. Suddenly she was being told that it belonged to someone else. Natalia slouched, willing herself to disappear as a rotund man in his 50's paced before them, examining the merchandise. Her heart raced as the man stopped before her, leering at those same legs.

"Siz," the man said with a nod.

Natalia looked toward the front door, her only path to freedom. Sitting lazily in a chair to one side was the man with the shaved head. A man she'd come to know as Dusan. The bulge in his right pocket she knew to be a gun. She turned helplessly look toward Ludmilla, who hovered nearby, warning Natalia with a bitter glare not to cause any problems. Lastly, Natalia looked toward the balcony and pictured herself plunging over the rail. They couldn't stop her from jumping. It was the only power she still held. But she couldn't leave Sonia behind. She couldn't desert her friend, not now. Natalia thought of home. The fields, the cottage, her parents and her beautiful little sister. She thought of the children, and of Vitaly, back from the army soon and waiting for her. She had to survive this, to see them all again. Natalia stood like a zombie and led the man down the hall to her room. As soon as the door was closed he began to smirk, like a child up to no good. Natalia moved to the dresser, numb to the fact that she was going through with it. She opened the top drawer and took out a condom.

"Hayir!" The man shook his head and waved a hand back and forth in the air.

"But,...herpes," said Natalia in English, pointing downward. She knew what she was risking. A beating or worse, if Ludmilla found out, but she was willing to take that chance. The man paused, disbelief turning toward anger. But then he looked again at those long gorgeous legs... She held up the condom and he nodded acquiescence, fumbling as he pulled her slip up and over her head. She felt the man's hot breath on her neck, the chubby fingers of his right hand running down the side of her torso. She smelled the stale odor of cigarettes mixed with perspiration. He stepped back to strip off his clothes, exposing a fat, hairy belly hanging over thin, spindly legs. An erection protruded from beneath dirty underwear. Natalia couldn't hide her disgust as he slid them to the floor, her face screwing up into a grimace. She took out the condom, placed it on top of his penis and rolled it down. It was only a mechanical act. It meant nothing. Like a trip to the doctor. Soon it would be over. She tried to disassociate herself from the moment.

The man threw Natalia to the bed and climbed on top of her clumsily. She closed her eyes and clenched her teeth as he entered her, the weight of his body heaving up and down upon hers, the bedsprings squeaking rhythmically. In her mind's eye, Natalia found herself in the fields on a bright spring day, singing with her mother and her sister as they ran their scythes through waving stalks of wheat.

Chapter Ten

"I'm starting to show." Sonia sat quietly, facing a bowl of thin soup. Across from her at the kitchen table were Victoria and Natalia. They'd lost track of how long they'd been in this place. Two and a half weeks? Three? Days and nights blended together in a blur, as though time itself had simply ceased to exist. They lived in a constant state of numbness, trying in vain to suppress their brutal reality, forced to service seven or eight men per day, sometimes more. If only they could shut their emotions off completely, perhaps they might survive. If they could cease thinking altogether. They were no longer human beings. They were flesh and they were blood, and that was all. This was the coping mechanism that all of them attempted but none could fully master. Inside the soul of each girl, the screaming and the crying and the sheer disbelief never ceased.

"You're pregnant?!" Victoria was aghast.

"Shhhh!!!" Natalia hissed. "Keep it down!"

"What am I going to do?" Sonia continued in a trance-like state, eyes glassed-over.

"Maybe you should tell them," said Victoria. "Before they find out on their own."

"No! I'm not telling them!" countered Sonia with a rare burst of passion. "I'm not losing this baby!"

Victoria pursed her lips, slowly stirring her own soup.

"I can't hide it much longer. Ludmilla might even know already." Sonia looked over her shoulder.

"Maybe we can give a note to someone," said Victoria. "To one of our customers. We could give them a note explaining the situation and ask them to take it to the police."

"And why would they do that?" scoffed Natalia.

"Some of the men are not so bad..." Victoria continued.

"None of them would tell the police about this place!"

"Then what?!" Victoria was wounded by Natalia's dismissive tone.

"We need to get our hands on a phone. We've got to call for help ourselves."

"But how do we get a phone?"

"Ask those nice men you were just talking about."

"I can't wait that long. I need to get out of this place right now!" Sonia seethed, her despair morphing into fury.

"You know what they'll do to us if we try to leave!" said Victoria.

"We need to come up with a plan," said Natalia. "There's got to be a way."

"I've been thinking about it," answered Sonia. "I have an idea."

"Let's hear it." Natalia grasped Sonia's hand.

"I'm not sure you going to like it..."

"Let us be the judge of that. At this point, I'm willing to try just about anything."

The first light of day crept through the window in the lounge, heralding the end of another long night. Natalia sat on one of the couches with Maria, Tanya and Sonia. Dusan sat in a chair by the front door, struggling to keep his eyes open. It was just past 5 a.m. and most of the girls were finished for the evening. This was the quiet time, when only a few drunk and lonely men dribbled in.

"I'm going to sleep." Tanya stood from the couch with a stretch.

The intercom buzzed and the sleepy Dusan flinched, opening his eyes wide to look around in confusion. When he regained his bearings, he pressed the button on the intercom to unlock the door at street level and then they waited. After a minute or so they heard a knock. Dusan unlocked the door and swung it open. A tall, stocky man with greasy dark hair sauntered in like he owned the place. Tanya sat back down with a sigh as Dusan closed and locked the door again.

"Is this it?" The man over the four girls.

"Take your pick or get out," Dusan answered testily.

The man eyed Dusan briefly and decided not to make a fuss. Instead he turned back to the merchandise, scrutinizing each girl in turn. As he sauntered past them, Natalia averted her eyes. She always averted her eyes, but this time there was even more at stake. They'd been waiting for days to spring Sonia's plan. So far the timing hadn't been right. Natalia knew they'd have a chance this morning, if only this man chose another girl. Tanya or Maria. Either one would do. Natalia concentrated on the far wall, willing the man to keep moving. He took a few more steps and then stopped in front of Tanya and pulled a pack of cigarettes and a lighter from his pocket. He took one of the cigarettes, lit it and inhaled. "This one," he said with a tilt of his head.

"Fine," Dusan replied. Tanya rose and led the man away. When they were gone, Dusan looked at the remaining girls and then at his watch. He put the keys to the door in his pocket, rubbed the top of his head with one hand and then moved down the hall, disappearing into the clients' bathroom.

"It's time!" Sonia whispered. She and Natalia jumped up and ran to Natalia's room. They pulled the comforter off the bed and threw it to the floor. Natalia stripped off the top sheet and they ran back to the lounge and then out onto the balcony.

"What are you doing?" Maria gasped.

"Leaving," Sonia replied. "Up and over to the roof. You better come with us."

When Natalia glanced over the edge she was struck with fear. An acute, immediate fear that told her she might actually die. Right here and right now. It was five stories straight down. She'd pictured this outcome since they first arrived, but either from being thrown or from jumping on her own. Somehow the prospect of falling to her death by mistake scared her even more.

"I'll go first," said Sonia.

"No!" Natalia countered. "I'm stronger. I'll go."

"Don't be ridiculous," countered Sonia. "It was my idea!"

"Don't argue with me!" Natalia snapped. "There's no time! I can help pull you up."

"Fine," Sonia relented. "But hurry!"

Natalia climbed onto the thin balcony rail, balancing on her two feet with her hands against the wall. The roofline was just beyond her reach. "Hand me the sheet." She struggled not to look down again. If she looked down, she might not go through with it. This was no time to waver. Above her and to the left, a short metal pipe stuck up out of the roof. It was one meter past the left edge of the balcony, which left nothing but thin air between this bit of pipe and the sidewalk below. Natalia took her sheet and carefully threaded it through her hands, forming a loop in the middle. She wobbled on the rail as she tried to toss the loop up and over the pipe.

"Natalia, don't do this! Please!" pleaded Maria. "They'll hurt you! They'll hurt us all!"

"Quiet!" said Natalia. "If you don't like it, go hide in your room!" On the third try she succeeded; the sheet held tight, looped around the pipe. Natalia gripped it with both hands and tugged, adrenaline beginning to surge through her veins. She could do this. For Sonia even more than for herself. Natalia gripped the sheet tightly and swung out over the edge of the balcony, hanging 30 meters above solid concrete. Her legs kicked as her fingers began to slip through the folded linen.

Maria held her hand to her mouth, stifling a scream. Sonia leaned over the balcony rail, trying to reach Natalia's right foot to help push her upwards. Natalia tightened her grip on the sheet, holding both sides together. If she let go of either side, the sheet would be released from the pipe and she would fall to her death. Natalia vowed to herself not to go like this. Not after everything they'd been through. With all of her strength, she bunched the two halves of the sheet together in one hand, releasing her other to grab a section above. Hand over hand she climbed to the edge of the roof. She was making progress, but with the sheet tight against the cornice at the top, she couldn't get her fingers underneath. "Where's Dusan?!" she called down.

"I don't know!" Maria glanced nervously through the door. "Just come back!"

"It's too late for that." Natalia thrust a hand over the top and clasped onto the pipe itself. It seemed an impossible task to get her body up and over. Through her mind flashed an image of herself, splayed out on the sidewalk below, bones shattered, body lying in a pool of blood. With a monumental lunge, she threw her second hand up and around the pipe and then slowly pulled herself upwards. For one brief moment, nothing else existed. Not the brothel or the sidewalk. Not the future nor the past. All of her focus was on this pipe between her fingers. On this rooftop, her singular goal. Her forearms dug into tar and gravel. She pushed one foot and then the other against the wall, gaining traction with her toes. Tapping reserves of strength she didn't know she had, over the top she went. Natalia rolled onto her back, eyes gazing upwards at the fading stars. She'd made it. She was alive. For a few brief seconds she stayed where she was, considering how close she had been to the opposite outcome. She rolled onto her side and peered over the edge. Maria and Sonia stood still on the balcony below, staring up in awe.

"You did it!" said Sonia, as though she could hardly believe it herself. "Now hurry, swing the sheet over so I can reach!"

"No!" countered Natalia. "Maria is right, it's too dangerous!"

"But you can't leave me here! You can't!"

"I'll pull you up from over the balcony!" Natalia hurriedly retracted the sheet and then moved along the edge of the roof until she was standing just above the others. She wrapped one end of the sheet around her right wrist and grasped it with both hands before lowering the other end down. Natalia spread her legs in a wide stance and held on tight. "Take the end!"

Sonia grasped the sheet as tightly as she could. She pulled herself just off the ground, legs flailing. "Maria, help me!" she shouted.

"Shh! Quiet!" Maria took hold of Sonia's legs and pushed her upwards.

On the roof, Natalia clenched her teeth and took two steps backwards, worrying that she might slip and go hurtling off the edge herself. Very carefully, she pulled Sonia up as she went. They were almost there... So close!

"Hurry!" whispered Maria. "I think he's coming!!!"

"I almost got it!" said Sonia.

Natalia saw the fingers of Sonia's right hand appear over the edge of the rooftop. "That's it!" Natalia's feet slid back across bits of gravel.

"Pull!" Sonia begged.

"I'm trying!" Natalia slid further still.

"I can't hang on much longer!" cried Sonia.

"Yes you can!" Natalia called back.

Suddenly Natalia felt the sheet go slack. She hurried to the edge and looked down. Sonia stood on the balcony below her, shoulders slumped in defeat. "I can't do it, Natalia! I don't have the strength…"

"Yes you do, try again! I'm not leaving you here!" Natalia quickly scanned the roof. There was a small air vent two meters further back. She could tie the sheet to that. Then tie another sheet to this one and lower it over. She could help pull Sonia up with her own bare hands. "Get another sheet!" she called out, but when she peered over the edge again, the girls were no longer looking up at her. They were looking into the apartment.

"Pull it up!" whispered Sonia.

"What are you doing out there?!" came Dusan's voice from inside.

"What does it look like?" snapped Sonia. "We're getting some air!"

Natalia quickly pulled the sheet up and out of sight. "I'll be back for you, I promise!" she whispered down, her heart breaking. When she saw the top of Dusan's shaved head directly beneath her, she froze, too afraid to even breathe.

"Where is Natalia?" Dusan demanded.

"She's gone to bed," said Maria. "Where we should be."

Dusan grasped the balcony rail and looked down. "Ok, get back inside," he muttered. Natalia saw him pull a pack of cigarettes from his pocket. He lit one and leaned against the rail to watch the emerging daylight. All he had to do was look up and behind him and he'd see her, too. At any moment he might turn around. Very slowly Natalia moved backwards, trying not to make a sound. When she was out of view, she stayed frozen in place. After a few minutes more she heard the balcony door latch close. He'd gone inside.

Natalia had to find a way to the street, before they realized she was gone. The rooftop was flat and nearly barren, with all of the buildings on the block connected to one another. Each building had its own small shack on top, along with a door. She hurried across to the next building and tried the knob. It was locked. She moved on to the next, hopping over the low wall between them. She wore only her green slip, with no shoes on her feet. Her arms were scrapped and bruised. But she was out. Or nearly so. The third door she tried swung open to reveal a thin stairway leading down into darkness. Natalia grasped a rail and made her way one flight below until she came to another door. Opening this one, she saw a button on a wall glowing orange. She pressed it and a dim light came on. She was in a proper stairwell. Around and around she went, hurrying downwards.

At the very bottom, one last door stood between Natalia and the street. She turned the knob and pushed but the door was locked tight. She rattled it back and forth with all of her might. It wouldn't open. Quickly, she rang the bell of the nearest apartment. Again and again she pushed the buzzer, banging on the door with a fist until a sleepy old man opened the door. He wore threadbare pajamas and slippers on his feet. His gray hair was mostly gone but what remained stood up in long, unruly strands. He squinted through thick glasses, trying to understand what was happening. Natalia pushed past him and on inside, hurrying to the nearest window. She threw open the blinds but the glass was covered with steel bars.

She turned to the man abruptly. "Let me out of here!" she shouted in Russian, but he merely looked on in confusion. "The door! The door!" She rushed back into the hallway to point. Suddenly the man seemed to understand. Natalia lunged forward and grabbed him by the shoulders, leaning close as she whispered into his ear, this time in English, "Open the door." The man nodded his head. Natalia let go her grip and he took two steps across the foyer and pressed a round button on the wall. Natalia heard a buzzing sound as the lock released. She pushed the door open. Before she moved through, Natalia turned toward the old man and put a finger to her lips. He nodded, holding a hand in the air to appease her. Natalia slipped outside and the door closed behind her.

The narrow street was eerily quiet in the early dawn, with no cars or passersby in sight. Natalia padded down the sidewalk in her bare feet, a few overhead bulbs helping light the way. After two blocks, she came to the wider avenue that she recognized from her arrival ten days before. Even at this early hour, small groups of men gathered on the sidewalks in front of 24-hour kebab shops and small markets. Natalia looked left and then turned right and continued on her way, unsure of where to go or what to do. The eyes of the men were all on her, luridly admiring her flesh. An old Toyota slowed beside her and Natalia looked over to find a man leering at her through the car window. He called out and then reached across to open the passenger door, nodding and waving for her to climb inside.

"You don't understand. I need the police!" she said in Russian. "Can you tell me where to find the police? Polis!"

This last word the man understood. He pulled the door closed, gunned his engine and took off down the avenue. As she continued along the sidewalk, Natalia realized that some of the men she'd passed were following her. Four of them hung back ten meters behind, matching her step for step and watching her every movement. She came to three taxi cabs, parked by the curb while their drivers stood idly by having a smoke.

"Polis!" Natalia called out to the stunned men, who merely gawked at her in return. One of the followers caught up and tapped Natalia on the shoulder. She jumped at his touch, spinning around to face him.

"Polis," he repeated. The man was thin and small, with a narrow, twisted face.

"Da, polis!?" said Natalia.

The man raised a hand and pointed. Further down the block, on the other side of the street, a car sat parked. It was white, with a blue stripe and the word POLIS written along the side. Natalia rushed off toward it, leaving her crowd of curious admirers behind. When she tapped on the car window, two officers inside looked up in surprise. They said a few words to each other and then opened their respective doors and climbed out. The driver was an older man, short and stocky. He hiked up the pants on his blue uniform and gave her a curious look. The other officer was taller, thin and young. He was handsome and perhaps a little less sure of himself; bashful even in the way he cleared his throat and tried to keep himself from staring too long at her body in that flimsy green slip.

"I need help," Natalia appealed to them first in Russian, but the men just stared at her blankly. "Help!" she repeated in English. "I need help!" She desperately motioned for them to follow her.

The older officer opened the back door of the patrol car. "Içeriye girmek," he said.

"Nyet!" Natalia responded, shaking her head.

The officer straightened himself, standing taller as he reaching for a billy club attached to his belt. He pulled out the club and used it to point at the back seat.

"No!" she shouted. "You must help me!"

"Arabaya binip!" he replied.

"But my friends!" Natalia pointed up the street. She took a few steps in the direction she had come from. The officer moved into her way, blocking her path and shaking his head.

"No!" he said. "In car! You in car!" He pushed her backwards.

The crowd of onlookers gathered on the sidewalk to watch the drama unfold as the younger officer came around to assist his partner. "It ok." He placed a hand on Natalia's forearm but she pulled away fiercely.

"No! Not ok! Not ok! My friends, they need help!"

The demeanor of the older officer took on a sudden intensity. He holstered his club and grabbed her left wrist, squeezing tightly. Before Natalia could react he swung her arm behind her back and spun her around. With his other hand he took hold of her right bicep and shoved her toward the car.

"Stop!" Natalia cried out. "Listen to me! Please!" She dug her feet into the asphalt but the man shoved her downwards and into the back seat where she landed in a heap. The younger officer slammed the door shut behind her. Natalia sat bolt upright and went for the handle but there was none. She was locked in. She pounded on the glass. "Listen to me, please!" Tears cascaded down her cheek. She'd come so far…

The officers stood on the sidewalk chatting nonchalantly. The older officer seemed to take no more notice of her, his anger gone. Only the younger one stole an occasional glance. "Drive me to the station, at least!" she begged. If these two wouldn't listen to her, maybe someone else would. A supervisor. A captain. Someone had to hear her. Someone had to help. The younger officer man made a comment to his partner, who shrugged and then slowly moved back around the car, opening the driver's door and taking his place behind the wheel. The young officer climbed in on the passenger side, turning to give Natalia a nervous smile through a Plexiglas divider.

The car pulled away from the curb and they moved slowly down the street, the driver rambling on as if Natalia simply didn't exist. They turned a corner and drove down a side street, watching as pedestrians put their heads down and scurried along trying not to be noticed. Natalia's anxiety grew as they meandered through the neighborhood with no apparent destination. The sun had been up for roughly half an hour when they passed the same spot on the boulevard where they had first picked her up.

"Where are we going?!" she shouted through a few small holes in the divider.

"Sessiz!" the driver yelled back. She didn't understand the language, but the tone was clear enough. Natalia sank into her seat, closing her eyes and praying that Sonia and the other girls were safe. If Dusan or Ludmilla realized Natalia was gone they would call Zigic. Goran Zigic. The misogynistic psychopath who "owned" them. She'd seen his brutality at work the very first day, when he'd raped Helena as a demonstration of his power. She'd heard more stories since. This was a man whose greatest glee came from inflicting pain on others. Natalia knew that she had to stay in the moment, to keep her wits about her. If only she could get someone with authority to help her, she might yet save them all.

When the car finally stopped at a run-down police station, Natalia felt a cautious sense of relief. At last they were getting somewhere. The younger officer opened the back door and helped her climb out, using one hand to make sure she didn't bang her head on the roof. Inside the station, a few more officers sat hunched over desks, hardly looking up as Natalia was led past. In the back of the room, a guard opened a solid steel door and then escorted Natalia on through into a chamber of cells. Prisoners sneered and made catcalls. In a far corner was another steel door. Her escort peered through a peephole before unbolting a large metal latch and opening the door. With a tilt of his head he motioned for Natalia to go on through.

"But, I must speak to someone!" Natalia pleaded. "Does nobody speak Russian here? Or English?!"

The officer pointed through the door this time. Natalia stood where she was until he gave her a light push on the back. She took two steps inside and he slammed the door shut, latching it behind her. "Please!" Natalia shouted again, but it was too late. He was already gone. In her daring escape she had succeeded in moving from one prison to another.

The cell was four meters square and filled with other women. A stifling odor of human excrement hung in the air. A hole in the floor served as a toilet. Beside it, water dripped from a rusted spigot into a metal bucket. Natalia's cellmates eyed her from seats on wooden benches lining the walls. A few lay sprawled asleep on the concrete floor. They were a forlorn-looking mix of homeless, drunks and prostitutes. A woman in one corner gently sobbed to herself. Another, aged and plump in filthy, ragged clothing sat leaning against a wall, snoring softly. Beside her was a skinny girl in a bright red tube top and tight black shorts. She had fishnet stockings on her legs and a languorous look in her eyes. Between these two women was a narrow space, not quite wide enough to sit. The girl sighed and made some room.

"Thank you," Natalia said in Russian.

"You're welcome," the woman replied.

Natalia squeezed into the space, trying not to choke on the debilitating stench of alcohol and urine that came from the sleeping woman beside her. Lifting her feet off of the cold, damp floor, Natalia held her arms around her knees and tried to figure out what to do next.

Chapter Eleven

"How long have I been here?" Natalia asked with a start as she opened her eyes. She'd dozed off, and without windows in the cell it was impossible to gauge whether it was night or day. Her muscles ached from sitting cramped between the others. She was cold in her flimsy clothing and she was hungry. Her only respite from thirst had come from cupping her hands under the spigot.

"It shouldn't be long," said the girl beside her in native Russian. "They usually let us out before they have to feed us, though you never know."

"But they haven't even charged me with anything!" said Natalia. "Why am I even here? All I was doing was walking down the street!"

"I suppose you were sleepwalking, not street walking."

"Are you one to talk?"

"At least I don't claim otherwise."

"I don't think you understand."

The girl looked Natalia up and down. "What's to understand?!"

"I was kidnapped!" Natalia thought she detected just a hint of compassion, but the girl said no more. The woman on Natalia's right stirred on the bench and then farted loudly, spawning shouted insults in various languages, none of which Natalia understood. The offending party merely crossed her arms and nodded back off to sleep.

"What about you?" Natalia asked her new acquaintance.

"What about me?"

"Why are you here?"

"Why do you think? It's all just a game. They pull us off the streets and lock us up every now and then so they feel like they're doing something."

"I don't mean why you're in jail. I mean here in Istanbul."

The girl seemed at pains to explain the obvious. "I earn more money in one night than I do in a month back home."

"Oh," Natalia answered. "So you came here by choice."

The girl's expression showed a hint of shame. "You have to get by in this world, don't you?"

"It was just a question." Natalia turned her attention to the rest of their downtrodden cellmates. How could Natalia Nicolaeva have ended up among them? And how would she ever get home? It was beginning to feel like she never would.

The prisoners flinched when the bolt in the lock screeched suddenly. The door swung open to reveal two new guards. Both wore the same blue uniforms and hats. One held a nightstick in his hand and looked around the room before using it to point at women one at a time. "Siz, siz, siz, siz…" He ended with Natalia's neighbor.

"I guess my time is up," said the girl.

"Ve siz," the guard pointed to Natalia.

"You, too," the girl added.

"That's it, I can go?" Natalia asked.

"You can go."

One after the other, the chosen ones filed out of the cell and on into the police station itself. "What is your name?" Natalia asked.

"Marina."

"Thank you, Marina."

"For what?"

"A sympathetic ear."

"Oh, no, this is not the place for sentimentality."

"Maybe that's all I have left."

Marina joined a line with some of the other girls to get their possessions back. Natalia stood beside her, unsure what to do next. What was going on back at the brothel? Surely she'd be missed by now. She looked around the station until her eyes came to rest on the young officer from the previous night. He sat at a desk, concentrating on some papers that seemed to make little sense to him. There was something about his demeanor that told Natalia he might be trusted. They were about the same age, for one thing, and unlike some of the others he seemed as yet untainted by life as a policeman. There was a kindness in him that Natalia recognized. But would he help her? Before she had a chance to find out, she felt Marina's hand on her shoulder.

"If you need anything." Marina held out a business card. Natalia took the card and looked it over; a photo of Marina striking a seductive pose, with one hand caressing her fishnets.

"Thank you." Natalia closed her fingers around the card.

"Good luck to you," Marina added.

Natalia nodded and then tentatively walked across the room and approached the young officer at his desk. The man was so engrossed in his papers that he failed to even notice her. Natalia cleared her throat to get his attention. When he looked up, he smiled lightly as he realized who she was. "Hello," he said. "Russia Girl."

"Yes, Russia Girl," she replied. "Does anybody here speak Russian? Or English? Do you speak English?"

The man gave a nod and held up one hand, signaling her to wait. He stood and walked through a door into a back room. Natalia heard him speaking to someone else and then he reappeared, motioning for Natalia to follow. She joined him in the other room where another officer sat behind a much larger desk. This man appeared to be in his mid-40's, with closely-cut hair and a military bearing. A nametag on his chest read E. Tozar. He looked at Natalia with suspicion as the younger officer continued his explanation. Tozar nodded and then gruffly dismissed the man with a wave of the hand. The young officer hesitated, looking at Natalia as though he wanted to say something. Was he trying to warn her? Or calm her fears? Tozar barked at him and the younger man replied timidly and then left the room.

"Please, sit," Tozar said in Russian, with a strong Turkish accent. He held a hand toward a chair in front of his desk.

"Thank you." Finally, Natalia was getting somewhere. Someone with authority who could, and apparently would, actually listen to her. Perhaps all hope was not lost after all.

"How can I help you?" Tozar folded his hands together on his desk.

"I was kidnapped," Natalia started. "A whole group of us was sold into slavery and forced into prostitution."

Tozar seemed unimpressed. "How did you get away?"

"Over the roof. I used a sheet to climb up. But the rest of the girls, they're still being held. My friend, she's pregnant! If they find out…"

"I can write up a report," Tozar said.

"A report? What is a report going to do for me?!" Natalia responded with venom.

Tozar shrugged. "How exactly did you say you escaped?" He fiddled with a pen. "With a sheet, you say?"

"You don't believe me?" She was incredulous.

Tozar sat in silence for a moment. "I don't disbelieve you. Where is this house, where you say they kept you?"

Natalia held up her hands. "I don't know. Near where your officers picked me up. The man who spoke to you just now; he knows where I was. I could find the house if you take me back to that place."

The officer pulled out a pad of paper. "What is your name?"

"Natalia. Natalia Nicolaeva."

"And where are you from?" He jotted her answers on the pad.

"Transnistria."

"Where is that?"

"It's..." her frustration showed. "Moldova."

"Where is your passport?"

"It was taken from me, when I was kidnapped."

"You know I can lock you up for failing to have the proper immigration papers?"

"I just told you, my passport was taken!" Natalia was losing patience. "Do you think I am making all of this up?! Why would I do that?!"

Tozar considered this possibility. "Do you know the names of the people who held you?"

"Yes. Goran Zigic," Natalia spat the name. "He was the leader."

The officer placed his pen on the desk and looked directly at Natalia. "Goran Zigic. I know of this man. You can take me to him?"

"I think I can find the house." Natalia allowed herself a small glimmer of hope. "I don't know if he will be there. He only comes around once in a while."

Tozar picked up a phone on his desk and dialed. He had a brief, heated conversation in Turkish before hanging up abruptly. "Come with me." He stood and led Natalia through the door. "Don't you have any shoes?"

"No. I left the house without them."

Tozar took her to the property room, where the officer behind the metal screen sat reading a magazine. Tozar explained something to him and the property man took a look down at her feet. He walked back along some shelves, picking through a few boxes before pulling out a pair of men's brown leather shoes. He brought these back and slid them through the grate. Tozar picked them up and handed them to Natalia. She looked at the shoes quizzically before sliding a foot into one of them. It was a few sizes too big, but it would do. She laced it up tight and then placed Marina's business card in the bottom of the other before putting it on as well.

Across the room, Tozar shouted a question to the younger officer. The man stood as he answered, looking longingly at Natalia as he did so. He seemed to want to come along, but was quickly rebuked and sat back down.

"Let's go." Tozar led Natalia outside to the street, where a small fleet of police cars were parked in a row. He walked to the newest of the cars and opened the passenger door for Natalia, who climbed in and sat down.

"We will go alone?" Natalia was worried. "They have guards, with guns. It is very dangerous."

"This is all the backup I need." Tozar patted a pistol in a holster at his waist. He walked around the front of the car and climbed into the driver's seat, then stared the engine and backed out. This was Natalia's cavalry, off to the rescue. She tried to remain hopeful, and yet, despite this man didn't inspire much confidence. It seemed that all she could do at this point was to hope for the best.

Chapter Twelve

"You remind me of my daughter." Tozar glanced at Natalia's legs as they drove down a busy avenue. Natalia pulled on her slip, trying to further cover herself. Weaving through traffic, Tozar gave an occasional short burst on his siren. "She's in college. In Ankara," he continued. "If she did what you do, I'd kill her. But she knows better. She's going to make something of herself. She studies history."

"You must be very proud."

"I think it is terrible. History," he scoffed. "Maybe she will meet a good man there. My wife, she sits at home all day. She is Russian. Like you. It is why I speak this language. I met her in the jail, too." He glanced back toward Natalia to gauge her reaction. "What do you think of my country?"

"I don't know." Natalia shifted in her seat uncomfortably. "I have seen very little."

"You don't like it?" He showed offense.

"It is a very beautiful place." Natalia gripped the door handle as the car bobbed and swerved.

Tozar showed a smile. "Yes, it is very beautiful. I think so." He slowed the car and stopping by the side of the road. "Is this where my men picked you up?"

Natalia looked out the window, trying to recognize a familiar landmark. The sidewalk was crowded with pedestrians and all of the shops were open. The road was filled with cars, honking and jostling for position. She saw an intersection up ahead. On the corner was a small store, where a man sat out front on an upturned plastic carton. "That market looks familiar. Go a few blocks further."

Tozar flashed the lights on top of the car and gave a quick blast on his siren as he moved down the street. Natalia's spirits rose. She was coming, if only Sonia and the others could hold on. If all went well, they would soon be free. The nightmare would be over at last. "Turn left here!" Natalia said, and Tozar cut down the small, narrow street side-street. She recognized the building, with the balcony on the fifth floor now empty. The sight of her place of torture and confinement made her feel lightheaded. "This is it."

Tozar pulled his car onto the sidewalk and stopped. "Which one?"

"There," Natalia pointed. "On the top floor."

"Are you all right?" Tozar looked her over with apparent concern.

"Yes," Natalia answered, "I'm all right."

"Ok, let's go."

"Me, too?"

"Don't worry. It will be fine."

"I think you need more men." Natalia tried once more to convey the urgency of the situation

"Relax." Tozar opened his door and hopped out. "These rats are not as powerful as they think. Especially when confronted by the law. They will not attack a police captain."

Natalia climbed out of the car more slowly. "You're sure about that?"

"I'm sure. Come. I need you to identify Zigic, if he is there."

"But these men, I don't think you understand, they are killers!"

"You witnessed a murder?"

"No, I heard the stories…"

"Do you want to save your friends?"

"Of course..."

"Then I suggest you come with me."

Natalia didn't like this at all. Her purported savior seemed an incompetent buffoon. Why wouldn't he listen to her? But then, she knew the clock was ticking. Every minute that she left Sonia alone in there was a minute too long. "Ok," she relented. "Let's go."

Tozar nodded. "Stay close to me."

Natalia followed him across the narrow street to the front door. Tozar reached up and pushed the top button on the column. After a moment the electronic lock buzzed and Tozar pushed the door open. He went through first and then held the door for Natalia. Just like that, she was back. The door swung shut, leaving them in the dimly-lit stairway. Natalia followed behind as they climbed the steps, Tozar breathing heavily from exertion. When they reached the top, they found the entryway unguarded. Just an empty chair. Perhaps Dusan was inside.

"This is it?" Tozar nodded toward the door.

"Yes. That's it."

Tozar gave a loud knock. Natalia took one step backward, ready to flee down the stairs if she had to. She wanted to believe this ordeal was nearly over but couldn't shake her doubt. Tozar was married to a former prostitute himself. Surely he knew the score. He had to realize there would be at least one armed guard inside, if not more, yet he showed no concern at all. Everything about this just seemed wrong. The door opened. Inside stood Zigic, arms folded across his chest. Beside him was Dusan. Natalia tried to bolt but Tozar was on her in a flash, gripping her in his arms and squeezing tightly. Dusan rushed into the stairway and together the two men dragged Natalia's thrashing body into the apartment while Zigic slammed the door closed behind them.

The men threw Natalia to the floor at Zigic's feet. "My little lost puppy." He lifted a leg and kicked her in the gut as hard as he could, knocking all of the air out of her. Natalia gasped for breath. From the corner of her eye she saw Zigic hand a wad of bills to Tozar, who tucked the money into his pocket.

"She says that one of the girls is pregnant," said Tozar. "I thought you might want to know."

"Is that so?" Zigic replied.

To Natalia these words were worse than any beating. Now her betrayal was complete. Dusan opened the door and Tozar walked out without another word. When bolt slid shut again, Zigic bent low and twirled a few strands of Natalia's hair before closing his fingers around them tightly. "So…who could it be? Sonia, perhaps?" Zigic jerked Natalia's head up until her face was inches from his own, his foul breath nearly choking her. "We'll take care of that. But not before we take care of you." He turned to Dusan. "Give me a cigarette," he said. "And a knife."

Chapter Thirteen

She lie curled up on the floor in her room, naked and alone. Knife wounds, bruises, cigarette burns; pain so overwhelming she could hardly distinguish the sources. Natalia pushed herself up on her forearms. Violent sensations ricocheted through her brain, nearly causing her to collapse. Blood pooled on the wooden floorboards beneath her. Natalia touched the edges a wound on her abdomen and winced. She'd been branded, the letter "Z" carved into her flesh. She had to stop the bleeding. Reaching the bed, she pulled herself up and then in, pressing the sheets close against her.

After a quick knock at the door, Tanya walked in. "I brought you some rubbing alcohol." She held up a white bottle, a bag of cotton balls and a box of bandages. Even Tanya, cynical Tanya, seemed shocked when she saw Natalia's condition.

"Where is Sonia?"

"I think you need to worry about yourself." Tanya eyed the blood on the floor.

"What have they done to her?!"

"I don't know. They took her away."

"Took her *where?!*"

"I told you, I don't know!" Tanya placed the supplies on the bedside table and then opened the bag, pulling out a single cotton ball. She unscrewed the bottle, pressed the cotton over the opening and then shook it. "You better not pull a stunt like that again. You'll get us all in trouble."

"Get out," Natalia replied through clenched teeth.

Tanya stayed where she was, a petulant expression creeping over her face.

"I said get out!!!" Natalia shouted.

"Suit yourself." Tanya put the alcohol back down and stalked out of the room. With hands shaking, Natalia summoned the strength to reach for the bottle and then poured the liquid directly onto her wounds. The shock of pain came with a flash of white light and she passed out where she lay.

The potent odor of rubbing alcohol filled her nostrils when Natalia awoke sometime later. She felt dampness in the sheets where the empty bottle lay beside her. The bleeding had mostly stopped. She forced herself to a sitting position and put her feet on the floor. Fumbling with the box of bandages, she pulled one out and tore open the wrapper. After peeling off the backing, she gritted her teeth again as she pressed it to her abdomen. One more bandage beside it and then she paused for a moment. It took a massive effort to stand, but she managed to move to her dresser, open a drawer and pull out a T-shirt. As soon as she'd pulled it over her head, she heard the front door to the apartment open and then the sound of tramping feet. Natalia moved into the hallway in time to see a dazed Sonia being carried past. Dusan and another man took Sonia into the next room and then reappeared in the hall without her. As he went by, Dusan stopped to face Natalia, leaning in close and pressing her against the wall. "So good to see you survived," he said. "We'll have to do that again sometime." He stuck out his tongue and licked the length of Natalia's cheek as she tried to turn her head away, closing her eyes tight. "Next time you might not be so lucky," he hissed, "but that won't stop us from having some fun." He took a step back and laughed before moving down the hall.

When the men were gone, Natalia hurried into the room where she found Sonia pressing a bunched-up sheet between her legs. "Oh Sonia!" Natalia dropped to her knees beside the bed. "What have they done to you?"

"They took my baby. My sweet Italian baby."

Natalia saw the color red spreading down the sheet. "You need help! You need a doctor!"

"Don't leave me!" Sonia pleaded, grasping Natalia's hand. "Please, don't leave me. I don't want to die alone."

"You're not going to die. But we need a doctor."

"A doctor did this to me. Their doctor."

Natalia looked over her shoulder. She could tell Ludmilla. They couldn't just let her die. Not like this! She looked back to Sonia and saw her face growing ever so pale.

"Please," Sonia repeated. "They won't get a doctor anyway. Not a real doctor."

Tears streamed down Natalia's cheeks. "Oh, Sonia, my Sonia!"

"Shhh… don't cry. I don't want you to cry."

"I'm here for you! I'm here for you!" Natalia put her free hand between Sonia's thighs, pressing the sheet tightly, feeling the warm sticky blood between her fingers.

"I know you are. I'm sorry. I'm so sorry…"

"Shhh!" Natalia exhorted. "Save your strength."

"I brought you here. It's my fault."

"No! I wanted to come. It was such a lovely dream."

Sonia forced a smile. "Wasn't it? Such a lovely dream." She closed her eyes and took another breath before the smile faded from her lips and she was gone. Natalia bowed her head and wept.

Chapter Fourteen

Natalia sat up on her bed, arms around her shins, knees tight against her chest. Her eyes were open, but her blank stare registered nothing. Her mind struggled to draw itself inward; to shut out the world. To shut down. Victoria found her, hours after Sonia's death, hands still covered with dried blood.

"Natalia." Victoria gently grasped her arm. "Natalia, speak to me."

Natalia turned slowly in the direction of the voice.

"You must eat something," Victoria continued. "To keep your strength up."

"They killed her."

"Yes. I know."

"They killed my Sonia. They killed my Sonia and her baby. Her Italian baby."

"Look at you!" Victoria examined Natalia's cuts and bruises. "We need to change this bandage! And these burns, you need some ointment!"

"I need to go home."

"We all want to go home, Natalia. They won't let us go home."

"I'm going home." Natalia was firm, as if the time had simply come. She climbed from the bed and moved to her dresser, pulling open the bottom drawer. She stripped off her now bloodied shirt and took out a new one, along with a pair of underwear and some jeans, then socks and a pair of sneakers; the clothes she'd worn on the day she first arrived. Clothes she hadn't worn since, but now she began to put them back on, struggling with even the slightest movement.

"Natalia! Listen to me! Don't do this!" Victoria pleaded. "They'll hurt you Natalia! Don't let them hurt you again!"

"Nobody will hurt me." Natalia slipped the clean shirt on over her head. "Never again." When she was fully dressed she reached back into the drawer to retrieve what little money she'd saved and then stuffed it in her pocket. Lastly she looked under the bed and pulled out the leather shoes she'd worn on the way home from the police station. She picked up the right shoe and peered inside to find a business card still resting on the bottom. After a quick look, she tucked it into her other pocket.

"You can't just leave!" Victoria began to panic.

Natalia walked out of the room and down the hall, driven by purpose, intent on one thing. She pushed open the kitchen door to find Tanya, Helena and a few of the others drinking coffee.

"It's alive," said Tanya with disdain. Natalia paid her no heed. She went straight to the counter, pulled open the drawer beneath it and pawed through a mess of utensils. Spoons, ladles, egg beaters… She slammed this drawer shut and opened the one beside it.

"Come on, Natalia. Enough is enough," Victoria begged.

Natalia finally spotted what she was after. She pulled out a large carving knife and gripped it tightly by the handle before walking out briskly the way she had come. Victoria still trailed along behind as Natalia marched through the lounge, past a few of the girls and a handful of clients. None of Zigic's men were in sight, but Natalia knew where to find them. She marched swiftly to the front door and pounded loudly with her free fist. All eyes turned to her, some filled with fear, others mere curiosity.

"This is the last time I'm going to tell you," Victoria continued. "Put down the knife!"

Natalia heard the bolt slide in the lock. When the door opened she was faced by a bored-looking Dusan. "What the hell do you...." he began to speak but had no time to finish. Natalia lunged forward, thrusting her blade deep into his belly. Dusan's jaw dropped. He looked down in amazement, as if he couldn't quite believe it. Natalia grasped the handle tightly and twisted. Victoria's screams pierced the air as Dusan dropped to his knees. With a kick from Natalia's foot, he fell backwards, gurgling blood, his eyes staring blankly at the ceiling.

Ludmilla burst into the room to see Natalia with the bloody knife still in hand. On the floor was her henchman, writhing in his death throes. "What have you done?!" was all the madam could muster.

"Come closer and you'll be next," Natalia seethed.

"You know we'll find you. We know where you live. We will find you and we will kill you. You and your entire family."

"I should slice you open right now."

"Go ahead then! What's stopping you?"

"I'm not a monster like you." Natalia moved past the dying man and dropped the knife on the stairs as she rushed downwards. When she got to the bottom she let herself out, pushing her way past a small group of sailors on the sidewalk before running off into the night.

Chapter Fifteen

"I killed a man," Natalia whispered into the phone.

"What? Who is this?"

"Natalia."

"Natalia? Which Natalia? Do I know you?"

"We met in the jail."

There was a pause on the other end of the line. "Who did you kill?"

"A man. Just a man."

"I'm sure he deserved it," said Marina. "Where are you now?"

"I don't know." Natalia huddled close to a payphone as pedestrians moved past on the sidewalk. She put a hand over her abdomen, trying to hide the red stain seeping through her shirt.

"What do you see around you? Are there any signs?"

"It's a busy street, with a tram line in the middle." Natalia looked up, trying to spot a landmark. "There's a big building on the other side with an Aeroflot sign on top."

"I know the place, it's not far. Stay where you are, I'll be there in five minutes."

"Ok," Natalia's voice wavered.

"Will you be all right?"

"Just hurry, please."

The cab pulled down a side street and continued along until Marina directed the driver to pull over. When they came to a stop she paid the fare and climbed out before helping Natalia. "Come on honey, you can do it," she said as Natalia wobbled on her feet. Marina closed the passenger door with her hip and the cabbie drove off, leaving the women alone on the sidewalk. Marina draped one of Natalia's arms over her shoulder and the two of them made their way to a door. Marina struggled with her keys but managed to open the lock. Once inside, they climbed the stairs to the second floor. Natalia was only vaguely aware of her surroundings as they entered an apartment. Marina eased her onto a single bed in the center of the room and then closed the door, locking out the city. "Let's get your clothes off and we'll put you under the covers." Marina pulled off one of Natalia's shoes.

"Just leave me," Natalia replied, "Just let me be." Her eyelids closed, her consciousness ebbing away.

When Natalia woke next it was in a state of confusion. She lay naked, face down under the covers in a bed, her whole body throbbing in pain. It was nighttime but the room was bathed in dim light, streetlights outside casting shadows through lace curtains. In the sheets she smelled the sweet scent of perfume. Rolling to one side, she saw the dark figure of a woman sat slouched in a chair across from the bed. "Where am I?" said Natalia, but the woman didn't answer, bound by sleep herself. Slowly the details came back to Natalia. She'd killed a man. Stabbed him in the gut and watched him die at her feet. Dusan. She formed the name with her lips. She felt no pity. Her beloved Sonia was dead. The shock of that realization was nearly overwhelming. She tried not to think about it. Not now. Not yet. Instead she listened to the sounds of traffic on the street below.

"I see you're still alive." Marina poked her head out from a small kitchen. Early morning sunlight filtered through the curtains, illuminating the room in a pale orange glow.

"But I wish I was dead," Natalia replied.

"Shhh…don't say such things."

"I should have killed him sooner. I should have killed him at the start. And Zigic, too…" Natalia was aware of the changes coming over her. No longer the naïve, innocent farm girl, she was becoming hardened. Forged in the fire of adversity.

"I'll make breakfast. Would you like some eggs?"

Natalia didn't answer.

"I'll cook some eggs." Marina disappeared back into the kitchen.

Natalia had to find a way back home. But how? No passport, little money, on the run. She tried to focus. She'd bought herself some time in coming here to Marina's place, but she needed to warn her family. Natalia couldn't use Marina's phone, it would be too easy for the police to trace the call. But then, maybe Marina wouldn't mind picking up an extra one for her at the nearest convenience store. At least nobody was going to show up looking for Natalia in Drosti anytime soon. For the time being they'd be looking right here in Istanbul. As long as she stayed in hiding and didn't make any foolish mistakes, she would be safe with Marina for a while.

Chapter Sixteen

Bundled up in a blanket to ward off a chill, Natalia sat on Marina's balcony on an overcast autumn evening, waiting while her hostess entertained a client inside. Pedestrians scurried back and forth along the sidewalk below, making Natalia envious of their freedom. Since arriving at Marina's place several weeks before, Natalia had yet to leave the apartment. She did get that phone she wanted, courtesy of Marina. Natalia had to let her family know that she was all right and that they were in danger. It was only when she had Ivanka on the line that Natalia realized how impossible it would be to properly warn them. What was she to tell them? The truth? Instead she said what she could. Things had not worked out as planned. She was coming home. When pressed for more details, she told them she'd call back soon. "Be careful," she'd said.

"Careful of what?" Ivanka was confused.

"Nothing... Everything." Natalia was at a loss to say any more.

At night Natalia suffered through terrible dreams, waking in a sweat, seized with terror. The ones where they came for her weren't the worst. It was the ones where they came for her family that made her not want to sleep at all. Sometimes it helped if she thought of Vitaly, longing to be held in his strong arms. She remembered the early days, when he first started coming by the house to drop off bouquets of hand-picked flowers on the steps. At first she didn't know who they were from. Vitaly was just another farmer's son who joked around with his friends and seemed to have no time for girls. It was her father who finally caught him in the act early one morning. It wasn't much longer before Vitaly professed his love; his deep desire to dedicate his life to her happiness, as he put it. Natalia laughed at these words, but slowly his persistence wore her down. He was handsome, enough. He was funny, much of the time. She was actually surprised at how heartbroken she felt when he went away for his army service. And yet, equally surprised how easy it was to get used to his absence. Now he would be back in Drosti already and after everything she'd been through, Natalia yearned to be with him. Vitaly would protect her. He would know what to do. If only she could find a way home. She longed to call him, too, just to hear his voice. And yet... they hadn't spoken in so long. She didn't want to tell him she was trapped here. She couldn't admit the truth about what these men had done to her. The shame of it was overwhelming, filling Natalia's heart with despair. Would Vitaly still want her if he knew?

The balcony door opened a crack and Marina poked her head out. "You can come back in, he's gone."

Natalia stood from her chair and walked into the apartment. "You're very kind to me, Marina."

"You'd do the same for me."

"We both know I can't stay here forever."

Marina answered with a look of sadness. They'd grown accustomed to each other. More than that, in Marina's lonely life, this was a bond she seemed loathe to give up. "Maybe we should give it some more time. Give them time to forget about you."

"They'll never forget me. Never."

"Of course they will. They have other things to worry about."

"I need to be home." Natalia laid a comforting hand on Marina's shoulder.

"What?!" Marina laughed. "Don't think I won't be glad to get rid of you!"

Natalia smiled and grasped Marina in an embrace. "You know I'll miss you, too."

Natalia sat on a chair in the kitchen, long bunches of shiny brown hair falling to the floor around her as Marina went at her task with determination and a sharp pair of scissors. When it was all finished, Natalia rose and walked to the nearest mirror. This was the first time she'd had short hair since she was a child, butchered back then by her well-meaning mother. Now she ran her fingers through it in wonder.

"What do you think?" Marina asked.

"Not bad." The cut was a bob, shoulder length with bangs straight across her forehead. "You have some talent."

"I didn't always work the streets. I used to actually get paid to do this." Marina picked up a small box of hair coloring from the kitchen table. "Black, like the locals." She mixed a packet of dye with another of developer. "You've never done this before?"

"No. Why would I?"

Marina shrugged. "I don't know. There *are* boys in that village of yours aren't there?"

"None who care what your hair color is."

"I suppose that shouldn't surprise me."

In the bathroom Marina carefully applied the mixture while Natalia closed her eyes, losing herself to the touch of Marina's fingers gently massaging her scalp. "Mmm...," she murmured, thinking back again to her childhood when Ivanka brushed her hair on Sunday mornings. She'd be home soon, Natalia thought. So very soon.

When the dye was set, Natalia rinsed her hair and then used a towel and blow drier to finish the job. She combed it before the bathroom mirror while Marina looked over the reflection of this raven-haired beauty.

"A whole new you," Marina said.

"Yes. A whole new me."

"We'll need a photo." Marina tacked a sheet up to a wall and then positioned Natalia in front of it. "Would you like to smile?"

"No. Just take the photo," Natalia answered.

Marina held up a digital camera and snapped three quick shots. "That ought to do it."

When the envelope arrived a few weeks later, Marina handed it to Natalia straight away. "I think this is for you."

Natalia carried it to the table. This was it. At last. Her ticket to freedom. She opened the seal and emptied the contents; one maroon-colored passport. Natalia picked it up and turned it over. "Russia?" she said. "But I'm not from Russia!"

"What did you expect?" Marina asked. "Russian, German or American. Those are the choices. I don't think you'd pass for those other two."

Natalia opened the document and looked inside at her photo, complete with short dark hair and a scowl on her face. The name read Alexandra Petrova, from St. Petersburg. Natalia flipped through the pages to find stamps from all over Europe. "This was somebody else's?"

"It's a passport, with your photo on it. That's all that matters."

"How much did this cost?"

"Don't worry about that."

"I can't have you pay for it."

"I'm not paying with money anyway. He's one of my clients. We worked out a deal."

"Oh, Marina…"

"Relax." Marina her fingers on Natalia's cheek. "It's what I do. Besides, we girls have to stick together. Sometimes it's the only way to survive. Please, just take it."

"Thank you." Natalia rubbed the document between her fingers; the wages of sin.

In the dim grey of early dawn, Natalia crept out onto the balcony one last time. She'd already been awake for several hours, worrying about the day ahead. She needed something to calm her nerves. She picked up a packet of cigarettes from a small table, slid one out and placed it between her lips, then lifted a lighter and sparked the flint, coughing lightly as she inhaled her first breath of smoke in the cool morning air. She returned the lighter to the table and sat in her chair, wrapping herself in the blanket and leaning back to watch the city come to life. Her mind wandered to the girls she'd left behind. How many countless others were being held in this city, dreaming of home and families and freedom? She knew she was just another statistic in a cruelly indifferent world. The image Goran Zigic haunted her still. Would he come to Drosti for her? And for her family? The man's pride was enough to suggest that he might. Surely he'd be girding for vengeance. Natalia had to get home to warn the others properly; to protect them as best she could before it was too late. She'd been hiding here at Marina's for far too long already.

The balcony door slid open to reveal a tired and dazed-looking Marina, dressed in a silk robe. "Couldn't sleep?" she asked.

Natalia nodded her head.

"I'll make some coffee." Marina closed the balcony door behind her once again.

By the time Natalia's cigarette was finished, Marina came back out with a steaming cup in each hand. "Here. Turkish coffee. Hopefully your last on Turkish soil."

Natalia took one of the cups and blew across the top before trying a sip. The coffee was still too hot to drink, so she cradled the cup in her hands to warm them. Marina took a chair across the table. Neither said a word for the first few minutes, until Marina couldn't resist one question. It was her last chance to ask. "What did it feel like, when you killed that man?"

Natalia turned her attention from her coffee. "I don't know. I wasn't thinking at all. I just did it."

"But what about afterwards? Were you glad that you killed him? Did it make you feel better?"

"No," Natalia answered, but then considered her response. "Maybe. I would do it again."

"Because you liked it?"

"Because it had to be done." A nagging guilt clouded her mind whenever she thought about it, but the guilt was not over killing Dusan. The guilt was for not having done so sooner. "I was a coward."

"It doesn't sound that way."

"You don't understand. I did what they told me to do. I let them use fear to control me, but I could have killed him from the very beginning. I could have saved two lives. Sonia and her baby, both. Instead I cowered in terror until it was too late..."

"Don't do this to yourself." Marina shook her head. "You're not responsible for what happened to your friend."

"I could have prevented it."

"No!" Marina demanded. "That's the difference between you and those men. You have your humanity. You're not a killer!"

"I am. First they made me a prostitute and then they made me a killer."

Marina leaned forward and clasped Natalia's right hand. "Sonia wouldn't blame you for what happened. You must know that."

Natalia was consumed by sadness. "It doesn't matter. I will always feel the guilt, for the rest of my life." The first rays of sunlight appeared on buildings across the street. A new day begun.

"I'm sorry. You're the only good thing to happen to me here. I just wish I could repay you."

"Go home and be happy. That's all I ask."

Natalia managed a weak smile. "You are an angel, you know. The angel of Istanbul."

"Please..." Marina laughed. "Come on, finish your coffee so we can get to the port on time."

"Stop right here!" Natalia shouted to the cab driver. They were just across the street from the ferry terminal. In one hand Natalia held her passport, in the other her ferry ticket.

"I turn around?" The driver was confused.

"No! Right here."

"Should I come in with you?" Marina asked as the car pulled to the side of the road.

Natalia shook her head. "I don't want you involved any further. You've done enough for me."

"Relax, it will be fine!" Marina tried to ease Natalia's nerves, but she couldn't hide her own concern.

"You know they might recognize me."

"Only if they're still looking, and I doubt anyone is looking. Nobody official, anyway."

Marina was right. Most likely Zigic would have kept the whole thing quiet. It was the kind of problem he'd prefer to handle himself. But there was always that chance. She couldn't rule out the possibility of fliers passed out to the immigration officials, with her old passport photo. Would a new haircut really fool them? Not if they were paying attention, but it was a risk she'd have to take.

"You get out here, yes?" The cabbie asked as other drivers laid on their horns behind him.

"I won't forget you." Natalia gave Marina a light kiss on the cheek.

Marina averted her eyes as her face went ashen.

"What?"

"I never do well with goodbyes." Marina mustered a shaky smile.

Another taxi honked loudly. "Ladies, please!" pleaded the driver.

"Good luck." Marina gave a hopeful nod.

Natalia opened the door and hopped quickly out of the cab. She rushed across the street through traffic, stopping only when she reached the sidewalk on the other side. She took one quick look back, but the taxi was already gone, blended in with the madness that was Istanbul. Natalia continued on her way with grim determination through the terminal doorway and down a corridor until she found a line of people waiting to go through a security checkpoint. Nobody paid her any attention as she got in the back of the line, the only one among them with no luggage.

When Natalia reached the front, her pulse rate increased. A hint of perspiration formed on her temples. They would notice, she thought. They would smell the fear on her. A dead giveaway. An immigration officer waited at a desk. When it was her turn, Natalia moved to face him, handing over her passport as she struggled to maintain the appearance of calm. He looked at her document blandly without a word. She would either be allowed through to the ferry or whisked off to prison. The man examined the pages, looking at the stamps and finally barking something she couldn't understand. When he saw her blank expression, he switched to English. "You overstayed your visa!" he said.

Natalia's eyes opened wide. "Yes," she answered, unsure what else to say.

The man stamped Natalia's passport anyway and slid it back with the haughty air of someone exercising the small bit of control he had over another human being. "Don't let it happen again!" he said. "Or we won't let you back in."

"Thanks you." Natalia carefully took her passport and tried to keep from running as she hurried onto the waiting boat.

Chapter Seventeen

As her bus rolled through the countryside, Natalia's emotions dipped and soared with the hills. Finally she would be home with her family, yet what would she tell them? Even more pressing, how could she possibly break the news to Raisa? Natalia still hadn't mentioned Sonia, even when she'd called home to tell her family she was coming. A deepening sense of dread pervaded her mood the closer she came to Drosti. In some ways it felt as though everything that had happened was somehow her fault. Natalia had dared to reach too high. She should have listened to her instincts and stayed where she belonged. That's what the townspeople would say, in any case, whether it was true or not.

Entering the village, Natalia saw the familiar storefronts, homes and schools. There was the bakery and the butcher shop. Raisa's restaurant looked exactly as it had, though it would never be the same. Nothing in the town itself had changed, but Natalia saw things differently. She was the one who had changed. Gone was her naiveté, replaced with a harsh and gritty knowledge of the darkness that lurked in the human soul. It was a knowledge that she would carry with her wherever she went, coloring her view of the world.

When the bus stopped, Natalia saw her family waiting. Her mother and her father, her sister, Olga and the children, all stood eagerly at the curb, craning their necks for a sight of their Natalia. She burst from the steps and flew into her mother's open arms, squeezing Ivanka tightly around the neck. She felt her sister's hand on her shoulder and saw the faint traces of a smile cross her father's lips. Gone was her humiliation, her fear and her worry. Natalia was home. It was only after she released her grip from her mother that she saw Raisa standing quietly nearby. The moment she had dreaded was suddenly thrust upon her. Natalia made her way to Sonia's mother trying to conjure words that might ease the pain, but finally broke into sobs.

Raisa's hopeful look disintegrated and a dark cloud crossed her face. "What is it? Where is my daughter?!"

Natalia grasping Raisa's hands in her own, gazing at her pleadingly.

"Where is Sonia?" Raisa continued. "Why hasn't she come home?!"

"She won't be coming home," Natalia managed, the world swirling around her as she struggled to explain. "It was the baby."

"What baby? Whose baby?" Raisa's voice rose in desperation.

"The baby that she carried. She…."

"What?! Out with it!"

"I'm so sorry! Sonia… She's passed to God."

With this Raisa let cry the despairing, anguished wail of a mother who has lost her only child.

Chapter Eighteen

He was leaning over Natalia in the darkness, his face looming just above hers. Natalia sucked in her breath, frozen in terror. "You thought I would forget you?" Zigic hissed. He brought a cigarette to his mouth and took a long drag, the tip glowing bright red. She watched, too terrified to scream as he lowered the burning ember toward her cheek.

"No, please, no!" Natalia sat bolt upright. Zigic was gone. She swung her head from one side to the other and back. Her sister Rita slept peacefully in the bed nearby. Moonlight shone through the window. It was a nightmare, nothing more. Natalia tried to calm her pounding heart. It had seemed so real that the odor of Zigic's musk and sweat still lingered in her nostrils. Common sense told her that he would never come for her here, so far away. But common sense was not a reliable indicator. Goran Zigic didn't operate on common sense.

When the morning sun filtered into the room, Natalia rose and dressed. She had breakfast with her family and then excused herself, taking her phone outside. She'd avoided calling Vitaly for weeks, first at Marina's place and now in the days since she'd returned. It wasn't that she didn't want to talk to him. She did, desperately. What kept her from doing so was fear. Natalia knew that she couldn't lie to Vitaly. She'd have to tell him the truth, about everything, and that was going to be an exceptionally difficult conversation. The time, however, had come. She dialed his number and then waited while the phone rang. When he didn't pick up, she sent him a text. *Hi, Vitaly, I am back. This is my new phone number. Call me when you can.* Later that day she sent another. When she hadn't heard back by the afternoon, Natalia began to feel concerned. This was the man she was planning to marry. By the second day his silence wore on her, a cruelty she could not understand. It was pride alone that kept her from running to him in person. After three days even that was not enough. Natalia simply had to see him. She couldn't take it anymore. With her father away in the Lada, Natalia rolled her old dirt bike out of the barn. She climbed on and used the foot-crank in an attempt to get the engine started. On the third try it coughed a few times and came to life. She revved the throttle, popped into first gear and took off toward the highway under a fading cobalt sky.

Light shone through the windows when Natalia pulled up to a stop outside Vitaly's place. It was a farmhouse, freshly painted the color of green fields. Vitaly lived here with his father, along with a dog that she heard barking inside. She shut off her bike's engine and waited until the front door opened. Vitaly poked his head outside. He nodded as though he'd expected her but instead of approaching, he stayed where he was in the doorway, holding the dog by the collar. He and Natalia stared at each other across this expanse that seemed to separate them, physically and emotionally. She lowered her kickstand and climbed from the bike. Her knees felt weak as she started forward, as though each step drew her closer to doom.

"Hello," said Vitaly.

"Hello." Natalia came to a stop below the porch, not daring to climb those few extra steps. Was this all he had to say? After so much time apart? "I tried calling," she added.

"I've been busy, you know." He looked at the whimpering dog in an attempt to hide his shame.

"Don't you want to see me?" The pain was evident in Natalia's voice.

Vitaly let go of the collar and the dog raced across the porch and down the steps to greet Natalia. At least somebody was happy she'd come. Reaching down, she rubbed the dog on either side of the head as he licked at her nose. Still on the porch, Vitaly ran one foot back and forth over the floorboards, then stopped to clear his throat. "I heard that you're a whore." He looked at her with the fire of accusation in his eyes.

Natalia's mouth fell open. "Is that so?"

"Is it true?"

"Who told you that?!"

"Everybody is saying it."

"And you believe them, without even asking me?"

"Because it's true. Isn't it?"

Natalia's blood ran cold with humiliation. She wanted to explain, yet knew it would make no difference. There were no shades of grey with Vitaly, or anybody else in this backward little village. There was black and there was white. She'd slept with men for money or she hadn't. It was as simple as that. Natalia was the whore, who ran off to the outside world and sold herself. Accused in the court of public opinion, she couldn't deny the charges. She would be a cautionary tale, told to young girls by mothers trying to keep them in line. She would be the one they snickered about at the market, whispering to each other, "Did you see her? Did you see Natalia over there, the prostitute?" Natalia was ruined in Drosti, for as long as she remained. Tears welled in her eyes but she fought to contain them, too proud to wipe them away.

"Bim!" Vitaly called out, clapping his hands twice. The dog trotted back past him and on inside. Vitaly took one step backwards and slowly closed the door, pulling it tight until the latch clicked into place.

Chapter Nineteen

"Father, wake up!" Natalia shook the old man's shoulder to no effect as he slept soundly in bed. She pushed a little harder and Victor mumbled some unintelligible words before opening his eyes to small slits. "Father, we need to get your gun."

"Gun?" his eyes opened wider. "What's wrong?"

"We need to be ready!" Natalia answered.

"Ready for what?"

"In case the bad men come."

Her father let these words sink in before he closed his eyes and pulled his blanket up over his shoulders. "Go to sleep," he mumbled, trying to doze off once again himself.

Natalia left his bedside and found her way to the closet, fumbling in the darkness. She reached up to a shelf above her head and let her fingers run over various odds and ends until she felt the barrel of her father's ancient rifle. She lifted the weapon off the shelf and brought it down carefully. Next, she reached back up in search of cartridges. These were harder to find amongst the hats, shoes and assorted clutter, but finally she felt a small cardboard box whose contents jangled when shaken. She took the box down and brought her cache to the living room where she sat in a chair and turned on a small lamp.

Natalia opened the cardboard box and poured a few brass cartridges into her hand, examining them closely. She wondered how old they were. This was the sniper's rifle that her grandfather had used during the war, when he'd faced off against the Germans at Stalingrad. It had not been fired more than a few times since, and only then at crows and the occasional rodent. Natalia ran her fingers along the barrel and peered at the wooden stock, the trigger and the firing mechanism. She slid a cartridge into the chamber and locked the bolt in place, leaned back in her chair and turned her gaze toward the front door. They could come for her now. She was ready. If Vitaly wouldn't protect her, Natalia would protect herself. She grasped the gun in both hands and settled in to wait.

The rifle was ripped from her hands in one violent motion. On instinct Natalia jumped from her chair, knocking her assailant backwards onto the floor. Only then did she realize that it was her father, lying on his back, rifle in hand. "What are you doing?" he asked, looking up at her. "You could kill someone with this thing."
"Yes, I know."
"Most likely yourself." Victor slowly climbed to his feet as Natalia took hold of his elbow to help him up.
"I'm sorry, father, did I hurt you?"
"This gun hasn't been cleaned in ages. You'd be lucky if it didn't blow up in your face!"
"I was frightened."
Victor looked his daughter up and down. "What could possibly terrify you so?"
Natalia wrapped her arms around him, refusing to answer.
"You're home," he did his best to console her. "Nobody will hurt you here."
Natalia buried her face in her father's shoulder. She wished that she could believe him.

Chapter Twenty

Natalia rode her motorbike down a dusty, potholed street between decaying wooden buildings, mostly vacant and deteriorating. They dated back to the Soviet days, but to Natalia these agricultural warehouses and worker dormitories were never anything more than a ghost town. High school kids hung out here, spray painting walls, breaking windows, and sometimes throwing parties inside the cavernous halls. There was one building, however, that the kids had learned to avoid. In fact, they steered clear of the whole block. Natalia stopped before it and turned off her engine. It looked abandoned like the rest, weathered by years of exposure to the elements, but she knew better. Everyone in town knew better. This was where he holed up inside, all alone. Trucks came and went on occasion, usually late at night, from the alley around the back. In the middle of the afternoon, all was quiet. Natalia leaned against her handlebars, trying to summon the courage to approach. The windows were boarded up, with some of the wooden slats hanging at odd angles where nails had fallen out. What might he do to her if she willingly wandered into his lair? He was a rapist, after all. So the stories went. Only Natalia didn't believe them. If she did, she'd never be here. She'd never consider actually asking him for help. But considering and asking were two different things entirely. Natalia tried to calm her nerves. She knew firsthand what men were capable of. After quietly watching the place for a few more minutes, she kick-started the bike, turned around, and headed back the way she had come.

"Why won't you tell me about it?" Rita sat beside her sister on the steps in front of their home.

Natalia plucked a blade of grass from a crack between the wooden boards and then looked up to scan the horizon. "I can't."

"You know people are talking." Rita's demeanor was solemn, as though she were sharing privileged information.

"They are ignorant peasants," Natalia answered. "Petty and cruel. They know nothing about what really happened to me. Only what their imaginations tell them."

"Then why don't you tell the truth? It couldn't be as bad as they're saying."

Natalia knew that she couldn't possibly admit to all that had happened. Who of them would ever understand? People knew what happened to girls who tried to leave this place. That kind of hubris was nearly always punished. Those without dreams of their own survived on the little scraps of joy that came from bearing witness to the misery of others. Natalia tried to tell herself that it didn't matter what people said. She tried to free herself from the shame, even as she dreamt each night of Goran Zigic coming to finish her. She knew in her heart that he would try. That was the only thing that truly mattered. When he finally did, she had to be ready.

Under a clear autumn sky, Natalia stood in a field not far from the house, squinting down the barrel of her grandfather's rifle at an empty tin can 50 meters away. She carefully pulled the trigger, felt the powerful recoil against her shoulder and then watched the can fly up into the air. She lowered the gun to examine it, rubbing her fingers across the stock. What stories did this rifle have to tell? What horrors had it seen? And how many lives it had taken already? That was during wartime. Her grandfather was defending his homeland from an invading German army. Natalia wasn't defending her homeland, she was defending her home.

"There was a scope on top." Her father's voice carried across the field as he approached from behind. "I took it off long ago."

"Yes, I know." Natalia opened the box of cartridges. She took out five more and loaded them one at a time into the gun. Her father watched as she shook the box and peered inside. "Is this the last of our ammunition?"

Victor nodded somberly. "You're a good shot." He eyed the cans scattered on the other side of the field. "Your grandfather would be proud."

"I never much cared for guns."

Victor furrowed his brow. This was hard for him. He wasn't the type for heart-to-heart conversations. He told his children when an animal needed care, or a field needed irrigating. Otherwise he kept mostly to himself, but now he seemed worried. "Tell me," he began. "Who are you so afraid of?"

"Bad men, father."

"What men? Who are these men?"

"I can't say."

"You are at home Natalia," Victor pleaded. "Nobody will bother you here."

Natalia turned to face him, staring him in the eye. "Father, I've done a terrible thing."

"What thing?!" Victor's frustration showed.

"We have to vigilant, all of us. Do you understand?"

"How could I understand when you tell me nothing?!"

She looked away, afraid to explain any further.

"I know that I haven't been much of a father to you, Natalia…"

"Don't say that."

"It's true. I left those things to your mother. I've let myself be a stranger to my own children."

"Don't blame yourself. Not for this."

"I'm trying to help you. I wish you would let me, but you must talk to me. Maybe if I had been closer to you when you were younger… Maybe you would talk to me now."

"I killed a man, father." Natalia couldn't keep it from him any longer. She couldn't bear to watch him suffer through meaningless regrets. "They forced me to sleep with men for money," she went on. "It's true what people are saying about me, but that's only part of it."

Victor didn't answer. His face went blank as he tried to process this information about his oldest daughter.

"These men, they'll want revenge. They'll never let this go. Never." She worried that her father might not believe her.

"But here, in Drosti…?"

"Yes, even here. Pride will bring them for me, and none of us are safe."

Victor looked back to the cans across the field. "How many will come?"

"I don't know."

Victor thought to himself. "We must explain this to the others. This is not your burden to bear alone. We are your family, Natalia. We will face this threat together."

To Natalia it felt as though a huge weight had lifted. He believed her, and even more he still loved her. With the gun in one hand, she grabbed her father in a hug, wishing that she never had to let him go.

Chapter Twenty-One

Natalia stood in the shadows, bundled in a long grey coat to ward off the chill. On her head she wore a dark Russian hat, flaps pulled down to protect her ears. Across the street she could see him, Gregor Multinovic, sitting inside at a table near the window, twirling his pasta on a fork. When he glanced out, Natalia pressed herself backwards into the doorway where she hid. She'd been trying for weeks to gather the nerve to speak with him. This man of ill repute was the only one in town who might be able to help her. She knew she couldn't simply stalk him forever. The time had come to act. Natalia stepped to the curb, paused for just a few seconds to gather her courage and then marched across the street.

Multinovic hardly looked up when Natalia opened the door to the restaurant and walked inside. A handful of customers occupied other tables. Natalia recognized the banker and his wife, eating their dinners quietly. Further in the back, two field workers shared a joke over a bottle of vodka. Natalia took off her hat, clutching it in one hand as she went straight to Mulitnovic and took a seat at his table. Too intimidated to speak, she looked him directly in the eye and fought the urge to flee.

"Good evening," Multinovic said in his gravelly voice. "I suppose you've come to explain why you've been following me?"

The blood drained from Natalia's face. "How did you know?"

"It is part of my business to know these things."

Natalia gripped her chair with her free hand. "What is your business, exactly?"

"Staying alive." Multinovic didn't take his eyes off her. "So answer my question."

Natalia looked down at her lap. "I need your help," she managed to get the words out.

"My help?" he laughed lightly. "You want my help?"

"What is so funny about that?!"

"Nobody here wants my help. Nobody wants to speak with me. Or to be in the same room with me. Nobody wants to live in the same little shithole of a village with me, but they're too afraid to do anything about it!" he raised his voice. The banker and his wife stopped eating. The field workers put down their vodka. "And you say that you want my help?" Multinovic continued in disbelief. "What could you possibly want from me?"

Raisa came into the dining room and stopped in her tracks, her mouth open wide as she stared at Natalia. "What are you doing here?!"

"Hello, Raisa." Natalia glanced across the room. "I thought I might have some pasta."

"Why are you sitting with this man?!" Raisa's voice rose in alarm.

"He looked like he could use the company."

Raisa stood where she was, a perplexed expression on her face, not knowing what to say or what to do.

"Are you all right?" Natalia asked as the other customers watched intently. The two field hands resumed their drinking.

"Yes. Of course I'm all right." Raisa retreated from the room.

Multinovic looked slightly amused. "See what I mean? I am a leper in this town."

"That much we have in common."

Multinovic shrugged. "I'm sorry to hear that."

"If your reception here bothers you so much, then why do you stay?"

Multinovic looked up at the ceiling. "I never said it bothered me. It suits my purposes."

"What purposes?"

Multinovic turned his attention back to his meal without an answer.

"You must be lonely here," Natalia said.

"I've learned to live with it."

"We are all social creatures."

"I used to think so."

Natalia detected the first glimmer of uncertainty in his eyes. "Will you help me?" she asked again.

"What kind of help are you seeking?"

Clearing her throat, Natalia finally came out with it. "I thought you might sell me some guns."

"Ha!" Multinovic laughed. "Why would I have guns?"

"Don't you?"

"You've heard conjecture. Innuendo, that's all."

"I'll pay you for them. Whatever price is fair."

"I have no guns. Besides, even if I did, a gun in the wrong hands is a dangerous thing."

"Only someone who has guns would say that."

Raisa came back into the room and placed a plate of pasta before Natalia along with a glass of cola. She gave a wary look to Multinovic before moving on to her other customers. Multinovic downed what was left of a glass of red wine and then wiped his mouth with his napkin.

"You're a Serb, aren't you?" Natalia tried to hide the hint of bile in her tone.

"What of it?"

"Just like Zigic," Natalia answered, mostly to herself.

"Zigic?" His head tilted sideways. "Which Zigic?"

"Nothing. Forget it."

"Tell me." His voice was intent. It was no idle request.

Natalia shifted in her seat. "Goran Zigic. The man who wants me dead."

Lost in thought, Multinovic raised a hand to his unshaven face.

"You know him?"

"I've heard the name."

"That's all?"

"Yes." Multinovic seemed annoyed.

"*What* have you heard?" Natalia pressed.

Multinovic said nothing more. Instead, he placed some money on the table, stood and walked out the door.

Chapter Twenty-Two

Winter came quickly to the Transnistrian countryside. Once the frost arrived there was little to do on the farm. It was the beginning of the long, cold season of darkness. For the family, winter was a struggle against both against the elements and the boredom. They had each other, but that could be a blessing and a curse, cooped up in a small house together for months on end. While she was locked up in the brothel, all Natalia could do to keep her sanity was think about home. Now that she was home, she found herself dreading the months to come.

"Your move," said Ivanka. They sat near the fireplace, playing a game of chess on a well-worn board with hand-carved wooden pieces.

"I'm sorry, I was distracted." Natalia moved a rook forward.

Ivanka immediately captured the rook with her knight. "It seems that you're still distracted."

Victor came through the front door, a cold chill blowing into the room with him. He was bundled in a coat and held a bag of potatoes and a jar of pickled beets. He also carried a small brown cardboard box that he laid on the table near Natalia. "This is for you," he said.

"What is it?" she asked with curiosity.

Victor gave a shrug and moved on into the kitchen. Natalia examined the box, blank except for her name written in a handwritten scrawl across the top. Was it a bomb? She wouldn't put that past Zigic. It would be an easy way to get rid of her, and her family too. She lifted the box very gently and examined it further. There was no postage attached. No address, no cancelled stamps. "Where did you find this?" she called out to her father.

"On the front step!" he shouted back.

"Who is it from?"

"How should I know?!"

Natalia stood carefully and carried the box to the front door. From a peg on the wall, she took her jacket and slid it on, one sleeve at a time, before stepping outside into the cold evening. A light dusting of snow covered the ground and a few more flakes drifted down from above. Natalia moved across the yard and out into the fields, walking a hundred meters before she stopped and gently set the package down. She took a few steps backwards and stared at it for a while. Could it be from Vitaly? No. Not after what he'd said to her. Not after he'd called her a whore. But who else? She came up with no reasonable answers. Perhaps she should shoot it with the rifle, she thought. If it *was* a bomb, that would blow it to pieces. Natalia looked around at the gathering darkness. Whoever left it could be watching her even now, yet she saw nobody. She would leave the package where it was until the morning. At least that would give her time to think. It could harm no one out here. Natalia walked back to the house.

The sounds of children playing woke Natalia shortly after dawn, shrieks and laughter echoing from the yard outside. She rose and looked through the bedroom window to see her nephews, bundled up in their winter clothes, playing in a deep blanket of freshly fallen snow. Natalia inhaled, reveling in the clean, crisp whiteness of it all. Winter had finally arrived in earnest. She envied the pure joy of the children, who lived completely in the moment. For Natalia there was reason to celebrate as well. She could finally relax, in some measure. The brutality of eastern winters helped wipe out the

Germans at Stalingrad. She couldn't imagine that Goran Zigic would brave one just for her. While the snow cut her family off from the outside world, it also kept that world at bay, at least until the spring. She remembered the package, buried outside in the snow. She would never find it now. Whatever was inside would have to wait. And if it was a bomb after all? The thought was worrisome, but as long as nobody stepped on it…

"What's going on?" a dreamy-eyed Rita asked from deep under the covers of her bed.

"Get up and see."

"Oh, tell me," Rita pleaded.

"Nope," Natalia smiled. "I'm going to make you get your lazy butt out of bed!"

In a moment Rita was up at the window too. "Snow!! Real snow!"

"Look at you, like a five-year old!" Natalia laughed.

"I'll beat you outside!" Rita threw on her clothes and shoes as fast as she could and was out the door in a flash.

Natalia took her time, to prove a point as much as anything, but she had to admit that the excitement was contagious. By the time she made it out into the yard, Rita was in the middle of a spirited snowball fight, taking on both of her nephews at once. A well-aimed shot hit Rita square on the forehead.

"Good throw, Constantine!" said Natalia.

"Hey, whose side are you on?" Rita complained.

"You can't handle a four year old?" said Natalia.

"Let's get auntie Natalia!" Rita shouted.

"Yes, auntie Natalia!" Constantine replied with a wicked smile.

"You be careful, Constantine! Don't over-exert yourself!" she said just before Rita and the children hurled a barrage of snow in her direction, the cold flakes hitting Natalia's hair and face, and sliding down her neck.

"Oh, you asked for it!" Natalia replied with a grin of her own before chasing the children through the yard as they squealed in delight.

"Why won't you tell us what was in the package?" Rita pleaded as the family sat at the breakfast table eating toast and fried eggs.

"I don't know what it is."

"How could you not have opened it?" Rita was incredulous.

"I'll bet it was from your boyfriend, Vitaly. Begging you to take him back," said Ivanka with a huff.

"No," Natalia shot back. "That's not possible. Besides, if it *was* from him, I don't want it."

"I'll bet you have a secret admirer," Rita speculated. "Someone who knows you're single again and thinks this is his chance."

"You are all very optimistic," said Natalia.

"So where is it, then? This mysterious package? And when are you going to open it?!"

"I am afraid that it will have to wait until the spring."

"What are you talking about?!" Rita was beginning to sound annoyed.

"It's under the snow."

"What do you mean under the snow? Where under the snow?"

"Promise me you won't try to find it!" Natalia snapped.

"Why not?" pleaded Rita.

"Promise me!"

"What if I stumble upon it?"

"I will find it myself, in the spring!" Natalia demanded.

Rita crossed her arms and pouted.

"You better not go digging around out there when I'm gone!" Natalia added.

"Gone?!" Ivanka perked up. "Where are you going?"

Natalia dropped her chin and looked to the floor. She'd been dreading this conversation, but now she'd let it slip.

"You're not leaving us again?!" Ivanka pressed.

"I'm only moving into town, that's all."

"Into town? Why into town? You don't like it here with your family?"

"I've decided to work for Raisa." Natalia looked up.

"Raisa…?" her mother let this information settle in.

"She needs help in the restaurant and we need the money, you know it's true. I'll live in Sonia's room six days per week. I can come home on Sundays." What she didn't tell them was how compelled she felt to get away from the farm, to live and breathe on her own.

"When will you go?" asked Ivanka.

"Today. I can use my skis." A somberness settled over the room. Moving into town was not far, but with the isolation of winter, she might as well have been traveling to the other side of the world.

When she'd finished packing her things into a large backpack, Natalia brought it out to the living room where the family was gathered, all except for Constantine who was nowhere to be seen. Natalia knew where to look. She walked to a section of paneling below the staircase and rapped three times with her knuckles. "Constantine, I know you are there. Won't you say goodbye to me?"

"No!" came a gruff answer from within.

"Please?" she beseeched him, but this time there was no response at all. Natalia knelt down and lifted the panel off to find her nephew curled up in a small hiding space within. "I couldn't go without saying goodbye to my Constantine."

"I don't want you to go!" he shouted as tears streamed down his face.

"I won't be far. I'll see you every week," she replied. "Perhaps you can even come to visit me in town. Would you like that?" At this, he bounded from his place and into Natalia's arms. She turned her head and kissed him gently on the cheek.

Chapter Twenty-Three

Multinovic arrived at the restaurant every Tuesday like clockwork. This was nothing new to Natalia. She'd been seeing him there for years, but now her perspective was different. After his refusal to help her, Natalia felt a rising bitterness each time she saw him. It was better if there were other customers in the place, to help keep her occupied. On this particular night she did what she could to entice the one other couple in the place to stay a little bit longer, for some coffee or dessert. Anything but leave her alone with that man. But when they asked for the check, there was nothing more she could do.

After the couple had gone, Natalia cleared the table, unable to avoid shooting a glance at Multinovic. He just sat there, glaring at her as though she owed him something. And why? What did he expect? At one point he seemed about to speak, but then thought better of it. Natalia took her tray of dishes back to the kitchen to wait him out. She knew that when he was ready, he'd simply leave the money and go. Then she could clear his table, sweep and mop the floors and head upstairs, done for the day. But ten minutes later, she was surprised to find Multinovic still sitting there, idly smoking a cigarette. He refused to take his eyes off her as she lifted his empty plate and wine glass.

"I'd like it back please," he said.

Natalia looked at the empty plate in her hands. "But it's all gone."

"You know what I'm talking about," he answered with a condescending tone. "You're like everyone else in this town. I thought you were different, somehow. Apparently I was wrong."

"And what does that mean?" Natalia flashed a hint of anger herself.

"At the very least you could show me some measure of kindness. Instead you ignore me, just like all of the others."

"I'm sorry if I hurt your feelings." Natalia was taken aback; shocked by fact that he even had feelings at all. Multinovic appeared unnerved by this tacit admission of loneliness. He fidgeted in his seat uneasily. It was almost enough to make her feel sorry for him, but then he sat up straight in his chair with a blank expression. "Good night, then." He stood to leave, walking toward the door and lifting his coat from a rack on the way. He put on the coat, zipped up the front was gone, through the door and out into the night. Natalia stood where she was, running the exchange through her mind. What kindness could she possibly owe him? The man had hardly said a word to her in weeks. She looked out the window in the direction he had gone, half expecting him to come back to apologize. But no, he wasn't the type to ask forgiveness. Natalia walked back into the kitchen with the dishes and tried not think of him anymore, but she was unsettled. She washed his plate, glass and utensils and then took the broom and dustpan into the dining room, trying to concentrate on her tasks at hand. When she was finished with her cleaning she turned off the lights and headed up to her room for the night.

Chapter Twenty-Four

Natalia woke with a start and sat bolt upright in Sonia's bed. He'd wanted something back. Of course it wasn't his empty pasta plate. It was the package! The package was from Multinovic! She let this realization sink in. He'd tried to help her after all, with some gesture of good will. And how was it received? With stony silence. The guilt settled upon her, but how was she to know? He could have attached a note! Natalia looked to the clock beside the bed and counted the hours until sunrise. She had to find that box. She got up and moved to the window. Outside, moonlight reflected off the snow-covered streets. She was tempted to go right away. Her Nordic skis leaned against the wall in one corner of the room. It was only ten kilometers away, but it was still very cold outside and if she showed up before dawn her family would think she was crazy. No, she would wait. Three more hours. She climbed back in bed and stared at the ceiling, trying to guess what might be waiting inside that brown cardboard box, buried deep beneath the snow.

Natalia felt the sting of exertion in her lungs as she inhaled the cold morning air and blew it out just as quickly, swinging her arms and legs in time while her skis cut new tracks through a thin white crust. She came over a small rise and she saw the farm laid out below, smoke drifting up from the chimneys. The last half a kilometer was all downhill and Natalia picked up speed, coasting all the way until she came to a stop in front of the main house. To one side she saw shovel marks and indentations. Someone was digging here already. Natalia reached down to unlatch her bindings and then bounded up the steps and through the door. Inside, Victor and Rita sat at the table having breakfast. Both were surprised to see her, but it was Natalia who spoke first. "I know you didn't find it," she said to Rita straight out.

"No. I didn't," Rita admitted.

"You were looking in the wrong place," said Natalia.

"So where should I look?!"

"Put your warm clothes on and you can help me. You, too, father."

"Help you with what?" Victor asked.

Ivanka stuck her head out from the kitchen. "What are you doing home?"

"I came for my package."

"Have you eaten yet?"

"I'll eat afterwards."

"No, you'll have breakfast first. Sit down," Ivanka commanded.

Natalia knew that she had no choice. She took off her jacket and hung it by the door before taking a seat at the table. Ivanka went back to the kitchen with an air of contentment.

Natalia passed out a ski pole each to her father, mother and sister. She compared their position to that of the house and then drove her own pole into the snow before poking it up and down.

"What if we step on it?" asked Rita.

"Don't worry about that, just help me look," Natalia countered.

Her mother and father lasted ten minutes before giving up and heading back inside. It was a fool's errand as far as they were concerned, trying to find some mysterious gift from an unknown admirer. Rita stuck it out, driven by purpose and the promise of romance. "You know who it's from, don't you? You can tell me," said Rita. "I'll keep your secret, honest."

"You'd probably never believe me anyway."

"Oh, come on!" Rita looked up expectantly.

"Gregor Multinovic," Natalia admitted.

"Multinovic!" Rita gasped in horror. "The rapist?!"

"He's not a rapist," said Natalia with a sigh. "At least I don't think so."

"I heard he was a rapist, and a murderer, too. The only reason he's living here is because he's hiding. Everyone knows that if they try to turn him in, he'll kill them."

"Come on, do you really believe that stuff? It's all just talk."

"You actually like him, don't you?" Rita was still in shock.

"No, I don't like him…" Natalia stammered. "That's not what this is about."

"Then why are you so excited? You like him! You and he…you aren't???"

"Rita! What kind of question is that?"

"What kind of answer is that?"

"I hardly know the man!"

"It hasn't stopped him before." Rita watched her sister's reaction for clues.

"That's enough." Natalia poked along in the snow. "Are you going to help me or not?!"

Rita shrugged. "If you want to date a rapist, that's your business."

After some time, Natalia felt her pole strike something unusual, almost as though she'd hit an air pocket, yet not quite. She pulled the pole out and knelt down to look in the hole. All she could see was snow and shadows.

"What is it? What did you find?" Rita exhaled plumes of frost with each excited breath.

"I don't know." Natalia dug with her gloved hands until she'd cleared a layer of snow from the top of the cardboard box.

"That's it! That's it!" Rita shouted.

"Shhh," said Natalia. "Keep it down."

"What for?"

"I don't know…" Natalia scooped more snow out of the hole. "Let's see what it is first." Rita dropped to her knees to help dig until they managed to pull the box up and out. Natalia placed it on the snow and the two of them sat staring.

"Are you going to open it?" Rita couldn't hide her impatience.

"What if it's personal?"

"Oh, come on!" Rita complained. "Just open the box!"

Natalia took off a glove and then used one finger to carefully poke a hole in the top. She worked open the brittle, weathered tape from one side to the other and then pulled up one of the flaps.

"What is it?" Rita strained to see. "If it's chocolates I want some!"

Natalia reached a hand inside and pulled out a note scrawled in a man's uneven handwriting. "For ammunition, come see me. G.M." Resting in the bottom of the box was a gun. Natalia lifted it out carefully. A black pistol with a plastic grip and a shiny steel barrel.

"A gun? What kind of present is that? Who gives a girl a gun?! Though at least if he tries to rape you now, you can shoot him!" Rita laughed.

"It's what I asked for," Natalia marveled.

"You asked that man for a gun?" Rita looked at her sister in disbelief.

"Maybe it's best if mother and father don't know about this. They're worried enough about me already."

"Can you blame them?"

Natalia looked slightly perturbed. "Just don't say anything. We didn't find the package, all right?"

"Fine, but if I were you, I'd stay as far away from that lunatic as you can."

"That's not your business." Natalia slipped the gun in her jacket pocket and placed the box back in its hole, covering it over with snow.

Chapter Twenty-Five

This time as she approached the dilapidated warehouse, Natalia didn't hesitate. In her left hand she held a brown paper bag. The other hand she used to knock firmly on the aged wooden door. A small security camera stared down at her from above. Somewhere inside, Gregor Multinovic was watching. After what seemed like a long pause, Natalia heard the lock buzz. She pushed the door; solid and heavy on its hinges. A dim entryway was lit by a single bulb from above. The walls, ceiling and floor were all covered in dust.

It was only once the door closed behind her that Natalia felt pangs of trepidation. The small foyer she found herself in was roughly three meters square. She moved ahead to another door, but when she tried this knob she found that it was locked, leaving her trapped in the dusty little ante chamber. "Hey, this isn't funny!" she shouted, but then the inner door opened to reveal Multinovic standing before her. He wore a set of blue coveralls, the type one might find on an auto mechanic. His tousled hair was uncombed.

"So you finally deemed me worthy of a visit?"

Natalia held up her bag. "I thought it might be a bomb. I was afraid to open it."

"A bomb?" he scoffed. "Why would I send you a bomb?"

"How was I to know it was from you? There was nothing on the box but my name!" she accused him. "You could have given me some idea!"

Multinovic shook his head and laughed lightly to himself. "You have a point, though I don't know why I thought it was a good idea to give you a gun in the first place." He reached out a hand. "Let's forget all about it, shall we?"

Natalia pulled the bag away from him. "Oh no you don't! You gave this gun to me. You can't just take it back."

"And what will you do without any ammunition?"

"If you won't give me any, then I'll find some on my own."

"Around here? Good luck."

"Why do you have to make this so difficult?"

"Because I've changed my mind."

Natalia's anger mounted. "You think that I can't take care of myself? That I don't know how to use a gun? Is that it?!"

Multinovic had a pained expression on his face. "Do you really want me to answer that?"

"Why *did* you give it to me if you feel that way?" Natalia kept at him.

Multinovic dropped his head, gazing at his hands while he thought it over. When he didn't answer right away, Natalia knew that she had him. After a few more seconds he looked back up at her with determination. "I'll teach you the proper use of this weapon on one condition. If I'm satisfied that you can operate it safely, then I'll give you the ammunition. If I'm not satisfied, then I keep the gun and the ammunition and you get the hell out of here and leave me alone."

"I'm not asking for anything more." Natalia pushed past him, moving on inside. The room was large and spare, with tall windows opening onto an enclosed courtyard. A set of oversized double doors was shut tight. Unmarked wooden crates stacked one atop another lined the left-hand wall. To the right, a portion of the room was modified into a living space. A couch faced a large television set. Four tall chairs were arranged around a matching table. A kitchen area had a refrigerator, sink and oven. The furniture and appliances were stylish and modern; unlike anything Natalia had ever seen.

"I know it's not the warmest of places, but it's home," said Multinovic.

Natalia saw dishes drying by the sink, crumbs on the kitchen counter and an empty vase on the table. It seemed so terribly lonely. She sensed that she was the first visitor to ever to lay eyes on this inner sanctum. A million questions swirled through her head, but she was afraid to ask them. She moved toward a bookcase, stacked floor to ceiling with titles in Serbian, Russian and English. Natalia reached forward and removed one, a hardcover edition of *Anna Karenina*.

"You've read it?" Multinovic asked.

"Of course. It's one of my favorites." She returned the book to the shelf and ran her fingers across the spines of some others. Dostoevsky, Hemingway, Victor Hugo. "This is quite a nice collection."

"I do have time on my hands, living here." Multinovic walked across the room where he slid a bolt and pushed open one of the double doors. "Please," he said, "Follow me."

Natalia pulled herself away from his small library and Multinovic led her through the courtyard, past more stacks of wooden crates. At the far end was another large door. He opened it to reveal an industrial-sized elevator. It was a giant cage, really, with a floor of worn wooden planks. Multinovic walked inside and waited for Natalia to follow. Her fears resurfaced once again but she tried to push them aside. She was going through with this; she'd already made up her mind.

"Are you all right?" he asked.

"Yes, fine," she answered, but her voice lacked conviction.

Multinovic rubbed one hand across his cheek. "I've already told you, I know what people think of me around here."

"I'm not one of those people."

"Are you sure about that?"

"I'm sure." Natalia walked into the elevator.

Multinovic shifted. The tension drained from his body. He seemed... grateful. With those two words, the dynamic between them seemed to change. "Ok, then." He closed the door and pushed a button.

"I'd like to think that maybe we could even be friends," she added. The elevator lurched downwards.

"Let's take things one step at a time." When they came to a halt, Multinovic opened the door once again and then reached out to the wall and flipped a switch. A long bank of lights came on above them, illuminating a cavernous subterranean space. At one end, perhaps 30 meters away, bales of hay were stacked nearly to the ceiling. Attached to the front of each bale was a white paper target with red bulls-eye in the center. Each target was riddled with a profusion of holes.

"Your own private firing range?" Natalia asked with incredulity, stepping out of the elevator.

"Whatever you see here, I would appreciate if you keep it to yourself."

"All right."

"I mean it."

"I *understand*," said Natalia, but then chuckled to herself. "And you said you didn't have any guns."

"That was not entirely true."

"No kidding."

Multinovic opened a cabinet above and thumbed through cardboard boxes until he found what he was looking for. Natalia saw rows of ammunition magazines packed tightly. He pulled out a clip and held it in his hand. "Forty caliber. Each clip holds 15 rounds." Taking the paper bag from her hands, he removed the gun and then slid the magazine into the handle until it locked in place, holding it out to show her. He flipped a release and took the clip back out, then did it again slowly before handing the gun and the clip to Natalia. "Your turn." He watched her carefully as she did the same. "That's good." Multinovic took the gun back again. "This weapon has no traditional safety, so be careful when your finger is on the trigger. Never point it at anyone you don't intend to shoot. The safety is an extra lever in front of the trigger, here," he showed her. "Like two triggers, first your finger pulls the safety back, then the trigger. It's best to hold your finger off completely until you're ready to fire. Stand over here," he positioned Natalia, facing the hay bales and handed back the gun. "Point at the target down there."

When Natalia followed his instructions she felt a rush of adrenaline, with her finger just off the safety lever. She'd fired her rifle countless times, so why was this any different? Perhaps because it *was* different. She'd never fired a pistol before. She was also being judged by her mysterious mentor. She needed to impress him; to prove herself worthy in his eyes.

"Hold the gun tightly. It will kick. Now disengage the safety," he said.

Natalia carefully pulled back on the first lever until her finger felt the trigger.

"And squeeze."

Natalia did as she was told and the gun jumped in her hand as a blast shot from the barrel, the noise echoing through the room, reverberating in her ears.

Multinovic turned back toward the wall behind them and took down two headsets from a hook, handing one to Natalia. "I'm sorry. Put these on, and try to use the sight when you aim this time."

Natalia put on her headset and then continued firing, feeling a little bit more comfortable with each shot, even as her arm began to ache from the recoil.

"Not bad." Multinovic eyed her grouping on the target at the far side of the room.

Natalia's heart swelled with pride as she took off her ear protection. "Thank you."

"Don't' let it go to your head. I'll give you four clips. That should be plenty. Next I'll show you how to clean it. Follow me."

Multinovic handed Natalia the ammunition clips and led her back to the elevator.

"What was this place before?" she mused as they climbed inside. "Some kind of warehouse?"

"It was a vodka distillery at one time. There was nothing much left of that by the time I got here. All the equipment was sold off for scrap years ago."

They rode back up and she followed him across the courtyard to a small workshop. From a drawer in an old metal desk he took out a small bottle of oil, a brush and a rag. Natalia handed him the gun. "Always make sure there are no rounds in the chamber. He removed the clip and checked inside. You'd be surprised how many people kill themselves while they're cleaning their guns."

"You still haven't told me why you gave it to me in the first place. What made you decide to help me?"

"I guess I'm a soft touch."

"I find that hard to believe."

"Believe what you will."

"Do you think it will make a difference? If they come for me?"

Multinovic paused, as if weighing whether or not to tell her the truth. "Probably not."

"*Probably* not?"

"I wanted to give you a chance, at the very least." He seemed overcome by sadness. Something bigger than Natalia. Bigger than this one gun.

Natalia considered his words. "I see. So you think I have one?"

"I'm sorry about your friend," he avoided her question. "She was a nice girl."

"She didn't think the same of you."

"I know."

"You were the father, weren't you? The father of her baby." The words hung in the air between them. She looked Multinovic in the eye, daring him to tell her. The sadness was still there, but the question hadn't surprised him.

Slowly Multinovic shook his head. "No." The resignation in his voice told Natalia that there was more to it than that. He was keeping something from her.

"Did you know who it was?"

"Yes. I knew."

"How could you possibly? When even I didn't?!"

"Believe what you want." Multinovic seemed annoyed.

"There is no way she told you about that."

"She didn't have to tell me."

"Somebody had to..."

"Nobody had to tell me anything! He came in to the restaurant one night. The young man. They got in a big fight. I saw the whole thing."

"Young man..." Natalia repeated the words. "Who was he?"

"I can't tell you that."

"Why not? Don't you know his name?"

"I know it."

"But what then? Why won't you tell me?" Natalia was exasperated.

"She asked me not to."

"She asked you? Sonia? Asked you not to tell me?"

"She asked me not to tell anybody. I promised her that I wouldn't."

"But she's gone! There's no reason you can't tell me now!"

"A promise is a promise," he said. "If she'd wanted you to know, she'd have told you herself."

Multinovic turned his attention back to the gun, using the oil and brush to clean the inside of the barrel.

"What did they fight about? Can you tell me that?"

Multinovic stopped cleaning the gun and looked back to Natalia. "He wanted to take her to Tiraspol, to a doctor there. The kind she didn't want to see. Your friend refused. She told him she was going to keep the baby." Multinovic took on a distant expression as he remembered the incident. "He was very angry. I thought he might hurt her."

"But he didn't?"

"No. I…"

"What?"

"I wouldn't let him."

"You intervened?"

"I made sure he didn't hurt her, that's all. He got red in the face and ran off, making some threats as he went. Your friend Sonia, she was strong. She surprised me."

Natalia looked away. Poor Sonia. What she'd gone through, all alone. It seemed the whole world was against her. And who was the father? A young man from the village, but it wasn't Ivan. She's said that much. Besides, Ivan didn't have the temper to make threats. Natalia ran other possibilities through her mind. There weren't many. A handful at most…

Multinovic put the gun back together and placed it in the paper bag along with the brush, rag and oil. He handed them to Natalia and walked out of the workshop, turning to wait for her. Natalia didn't move. It stung that this man, this near total stranger, knew more about Sonia than she did.

"That's all I can tell you. After what happened I thought that she might be a little kinder to me, but… maybe I expected too much." Multinovic walked on and this time Natalia followed him into his living area.

"I'm sorry she didn't treat you better."

"I never blamed her." Multinovic opened the front door and stood aside to let Natalia out.

"Is that all?"

"What else do you want?" He seemed perplexed.

"I thought maybe we could have some tea."

"Tea?" He said the word as though he'd never heard of such a thing.

"Yes, tea. You do drink tea, don't you?"

"You want to have tea with me?"

"Why not?"

Multinovic frowned. He seemed more surprised at this question than at any of the others she'd asked so far, as though the concept of someone choosing to spend time with him was one he couldn't quite comprehend. "All right. We could have some tea." He eyed her carefully, pushing aside his incredulity.

Natalia placed her paper bag on the dining table and took a seat. She watched as Multinovic moved across the room and into the kitchen area where he thumbed through a selection of teas arranged on a wooden shelf. "Any preference?" he asked. "Green, black, herbal…"

"Black, please."

Multinovic put one of the boxes on the counter, then took an electric kettle and filled it with water before placing it in a cradle. "Milk and sugar?"

"Yes, both."

Multinovic took two mugs from another cabinet and put them on the table, along with a bowl of sugar. When he opened the refrigerator, Natalia managed a peek inside. She saw vegetables, some cheese and a few white-paper packages that would have come from the butcher. Multinovic pulled out a glass milk bottle and put it on the table next to the sugar.

"Who does your shopping?" Natalia asked.

"I do. Who else?"

"I don't know. I've never seen you around the village except at the restaurant. You seem to spend a lot of time here at home."

"I get out," he seemed offended. "From time to time."

"It must be hard for you, without any friends here."

"I manage."

"That doesn't mean it isn't difficult. Don't you get lonely?"

He took two tea bags from the box and handed one of them to Natalia. "I try not to think about it."

"How can you not think about it? Sitting here by yourself, day after day? Don't you have family somewhere?"

"Is this why you wanted to have tea?" Multinovic took his teabag from its paper sleeve and lowered it into his mug. "To question me about my personal life?"

"I don't mean to overstep my bounds. I'm just curious." Natalia wondered if this was such a good idea after all. Perhaps she should just go. She cleared her throat, about to say so, when the kettle let out a siren wail. Multinovic lifted it from its cradle and then poured the steaming hot water into Natalia's mug first and then his own. She lowered in her tea bag, bouncing it lightly up and down, watching the color escape in a swirl of circles.

"You're right that it hasn't been easy. Living here, I mean."

Natalia blew on her tea and remained silent, afraid to pry any further.

"Sometimes I think I might go mad, to be honest."

"I know I couldn't do it. All alone like this..."

Multinovic cleared his throat, as though searching for a response. She wondered if he might actually *want* to talk about these things. Most likely this was his first social visit in as long as he'd lived in the village, and that was several years. She knew better than to coax him too hard. Perhaps if she simply let him guide the conversation some fragments of his story might spill out.

"My life wasn't always this way," he said.

"No, I wouldn't suspect that it was."

Multinovic drifted off a little, thinking of days long past. "I was young once, like you, full of dreams. Nothing extraordinary, of course, but I never expected this."

"What did you expect?"

He rubbed one finger along his chin. There was a faraway look in his eyes. Natalia wasn't sure if she was witnessing sadness or merely introspection. "I was a mechanic's apprentice for the national railways. I thought I would make a career out of it. You know, forty-five years and then a pension. Maybe a wife and a few kids along the way. Holidays on the Adriatic sea."

"So what happened?"

He leaned back in his chair and rolled his eyes. "We had a war. Maybe you heard about it."

"I heard about it, but that was before I was born."

"Well, it was the end of my plans."

"But that war is over. It's been over for a long time, more than twenty years! Perhaps somebody told you?"

Multinovic glared at her. "I am aware of that."

"Were you injured? You seem fine to me."

"Thank you for your appraisal."

"A lot of people fought in that war. They're not all living in Transnistria, smuggling weapons for a living."

"No, some of them are living in Istanbul, smuggling women."

Natalia put her mug down on the table, the edges of the room receding into a fog. "You knew him?"

Multinovic looked away, seeming to regret his words. "Yes. I knew him."

"Tell me." Natalia was done cozying up. "Everything."

"He is a cold-blooded killer and a psychopath. What more is there to tell?"

"Are you running from him, too?"

"No. I would never run from that man."

"What then?"

"I suppose you could say I'm running from what he did to me. To my reputation."

"The time for secrets between us is over, Gregor. Please show me the respect of a full and honest answer. I think I deserve that much."

"Gregor," he repeated his own name. "Nobody has called me that in a very long time."

"Please…"

"We served together, in the war," he said. "We belonged to the same unit."

"So you knew him well?"

"Too well. A man like this in wartime is a very dangerous thing."

"A man like Zigic is dangerous any time, in peace or in war."

"Yes, but in war his behavior is not only accepted, it is encouraged. He is given weapons and the stamp of authority. He is sent into the field and told to rape and to pillage and to murder."

"But those are not the rules of war."

"No. Not the rules, but the reality. Our reality, anyway."

"You were ordered to rape? To murder?" Natalia felt the blood draining from her fingertips and her toes.

"Ordered, yes."

"And?"

"They were orders that I would never follow, but I certainly couldn't stop Zigic."

Natalia saw the guilt in his eyes and in the way his shoulders slumped. "Why run then, if your own conscience is clear? If your only crime was to silently bear witness?"

"When the war ended, the entire unit was charged with war crimes. I was a wanted man. I had to run, don't you see? I was forced to run. So I went into business. The only business I really knew by that point."

"But they can't be searching for war criminals any longer? Why don't you just go home? Why are you still here?"

Multinovic laughed to himself. "You're right that the Hague has no interest in me anymore. Now I'm wanted as a weapons smuggler. There are very few places I can live at this point without being arrested. Besides, I make a decent living here. There is plenty of product to be had in this region and government officials that are amenable to my business-model. No end to customers, either."

"What customers? Nobody is fighting around here."

"These days it's mostly Ukraine, both sides. But also, Kurdistan is not so far. Lebanon, Syria, Afghanistan. As long as I can arrange the transport I usually don't have to go anywhere myself. Sometimes I take the goods as far as the Black Sea, but that's it. I'm back in a few days."

"And you call this a life?"

Multinovic lowered his eyes. "No. Not hardly."

"So why don't you do something else? Get married? Have some children? Holidays on the Adriatic Sea?"

Multinovic laughed again. "I think it's too late for all of that. Perhaps a nice quiet life in Argentina, though."

Natalia breathed in deeply and exhaled. "So that's it, then? The mystery of Gregor Multinovic finally solved."

"I hope you will have to decency to keep this information to yourself."

"On one condition."

"I'm not in the habit of accepting conditions."

"Maybe you should have thought of that beforehand."

"Yes, well, what are your conditions?"

"I want you to teach me."

"Teach you what?"

"Everything. How to fight, how to use a knife, how to defend myself with household appliances, whatever you think might be of use."

"And what do I get out of it, aside from your purported vow of silence, which I think you owe me anyway?"

"Somebody to talk to now and then."

"You're selling your friendship? Is that it?" He took offense.

"No," she shook her head in regret. "That comes free, regardless. If you don't want to help me, I understand. Your secrets are safe."

Multinovic licked his lower lip. "There are some things I could teach you, I suppose."

A light smile showed at the corners of Natalia's mouth. "All right, then. It's settled." At these words he seemed almost happy. She leaned back in her seat and took another small sip of tea. It seemed that Sonia had this man all wrong. Despite his questionable history, perhaps Gregor Mulitnovic was not such a bad guy after all.

Chapter Twenty-Six

She stood at the counter of the local butcher shop waiting for her order to be filled, flexing her right bicep as she ran her left hand across the bulge of muscle. Natalia was always a strong girl, working on the farm, but now her muscles were becoming even more toned and firm. She was an athlete in training, running each morning at dawn and then pushing herself for an hour more in a private gym at Multinovic's place. In the past three months, she'd learned more than she ever could have imagined. She could disassemble, assemble and fire various machine guns, assault rifles and even a rocket-propelled grenade launcher. She'd had lessons in explosives, navigation and communications electronics. The equipment Multinovic had on hand ranged from night-vision goggles to GPS units to eavesdropping gear. He was a one-stop shop for battlefield supplies and she knew how to operate them all.

The lesson Natalia looked forward to the most each day was her afternoon session in martial arts. According to Mulitnovic, she had a natural ability. When it came to brute strength she was no match for him, but she made up for that with speed, flexibility and creativity. Each day she came just a little bit closer to beating him. She could already hold her own. If she ever got this close to Zigic or his men, she'd stand a decent chance.

When the butcher put the last of three wrapped packages in a bag on the counter, Natalia paid the total. She hefted the bag and walked out onto a wood-plank sidewalk, turning left toward the restaurant. A weak sun shone for the first time in nearly a month and snow on the unpaved street melted into thick mud. She reached an intersection and stopped, searching the road for the clearest path. From directly behind her, Natalia felt a presence even before she heard the long, low whistle. She'd become used to taunts and jeers from the villagers. It started with the rumors of her time abroad and then grew with the gossip about Multinovic. Everybody knew she spent her time with him. It wasn't the kind of thing you could hide in a place like Drosti. They were outcasts together at this point. Against her better instincts, Natalia turned to face her accusers. She saw Vitaly sitting in a doorway nearby, loitering with two of his childhood friends; Nikola, the suave-looking banker's son who thought himself a ladies' man and Boris, a rangy redhead with a hungry, malevolent look in his eye. She'd known these boys all of her life, usually doing her best to avoid them. She hadn't had to avoid Vitaly lately, seeing him only twice in three months. Both previous times he merely turned and walked the other way. This time he stayed put, a sly smile on his lips.

"Look who we have here," said Boris, "Your girlfriend, the prostitute."

"Maybe we can have some fun this afternoon. I always wanted a piece of that," said Nikola.

Vitaly remained quiet, arms crossed as he eyed Natalia. She turned her back on the three of them and waited as a delivery truck lumbered past down the street. The right rear wheel hit a deep puddle, sending a stream of mud across Natalia's feet and soaking her pants and shoes.

"Oh, look, the dirty girl got dirty!" Boris climbed to his feet and approached her.

"Haven't you anything better to do than hang around harassing people?" Natalia shot back.

"Uh oh, I think we've upset her!" Nikola flashed a wicked smile, joining Boris to block her way. "You're not going to raise your rates on us, are you? Because we heard you were very cheap."

"Yes, dirt cheap," said Boris.

"Your friends are clever boys, aren't they Vitaly?" Natalia looked in his direction.

"You're one to talk." Vitaly rose slowly and sauntered toward her, an arrogance in his step. "At least none of us are fucking the Serb."

"Take that back." Natalia struggling to restrain herself.

"Why should I?!" He stuck out his chest and tilted his head slightly, as if to intimidate her.

"Are you jealous?" she pressed him.

"Ha! You two were made for each other. A criminal and a common whore."

Natalia wouldn't let him get to her. He simply wasn't worth it. She turned her back on Vitaly and pushed past the others. As she took her first step off the sidewalk, a shove from behind sent her flying forward and down face-first into the mud, her bag of meat landing with a thud beside her. Natalia lay where she was for a moment in sheer disbelief. Had Vitaly done that? The man she'd planned to marry? She rolled over and looked up to see the three of them standing on the wood planks above her. Boris and Nikola laughed while Vitaly merely stared down at her. "Go fuck your Serb now," he said. "I'll bet *he* likes it dirty."

Natalia sat up and examined herself. Mud on her arms and legs, face and clothing.

"Too bad Sonia didn't come back with her," Boris said. "I'll bet she liked it dirty, too, didn't she Nikola?"

"Shut up," Nikola quietly seethed.

"I'm just saying…" Boris laughed.

"I said shut up!" Nikola cut him off. There was something in the *way* he said it that made Natalia take notice. The way he bristled at the mention of Sonia's name. The way he seemed to take it personally. Natalia looked him up and down and it all made sense. Not a bad-looking boy. His family had some money. Why hadn't she seen it before? Natalia climbed to her feet. "It was you," she said, staring straight at him. "I should have known."

"You know nothing," Nikola replied, but his swagger was gone.

"It was your baby she died for."

"What baby? There was no baby…"

Natalia shook her head. "Don't lie to me, Nikola. I already know. At least you got what you wanted, though. There's no baby now. You don't have to worry about that anymore." Natalia saw what looked like remorse cross Nikola's face.

"Go back to your Serb and leave us alone?" said Vitaly.

"Leave *you* alone? Am I bothering you?" Natalia retrieved her bag and placed it on the sidewalk before climbing up after. "I'll leave you alone when I'm finished with you. Once I've taught you some respect." She stood before Vitaly, noting the smugness that still smoldered in his eyes. He barely had time to laugh before she hit him hard with an open-hand to the side of his smirking face. In one continuous motion she swung her left leg, taking both of his out from under him. He landed hard on the planks and she kicked him off the sidewalk into the mud himself. Boris' mouth dropped open before Natalia swung an elbow into his gut, knocking him into the street with one blow.

Nikola was the last to face her, flexing his muscles as he prepared himself for a fight. He swung first at her muddy face, but Natalia ducked to her left and then caught him with a blow to the chest, knocking the wind out of him. She grabbed his jacket with both hands and threw him after the others into the mud below. "Look at that. Beaten by a common whore. What a shame." She reached down to pick up her bag of meat. Natalia walked past them and made her way up the block, feeling a sense of exhilaration tempered by her newfound knowledge. She never should have suspected Multinovic, but in the end the identity of the father made little difference. Sonia was gone. That pain would never leave Natalia, but when she pictured those three faces as the boys lay in the street, wallowing in mud and beaten by a girl, she couldn't help but feel a sense of pride. It was as though she'd taken vengeance on the whole town. The old women clucking their tongues and the mothers shooing their children away from her, as if her shame were some deadly virus. The men who stared at her like she was common property. Let's see how they looked at her now, she thought.

"What have you done!?" Raisa gasped when Natalia entered the restaurant, dripping mud from head to toe.

"I'm sorry. I'll wash it."

"Go wash yourself!" Raisa took the package from her hand. "Look at you, you're tracking dirt everywhere! Take those shoes off!" She shook her head and muttered to herself as she disappeared into the kitchen to salvage her meat.

Chapter Twenty-Seven

Multinovic stood looking in the mirror at the reflection of a wrinkled old woman beside him. Spread out on a table before them was an array of makeup, plastic and rubber. "What do you think of me?" the woman croaked.

"Not bad," Multinovic answered. "Most people tend to over-do it the first few times. They stand out in a crowd because they try too hard. You've shown a good deal of restraint. Very life-like."

"Thank you," Natalia answered in her normal voice. "Maybe I should show up to work at the café like this."

"Not unless you want to give Raisa a heart attack" Multinovic offered an easy smile. They'd grown close in the months since she'd started her training. Perhaps even *too* close. Sometimes in the mornings, when they worked out together on the exercise equipment, Natalia found herself staring at his figure just a few seconds too long. The lightest touch sent previously unknown emotions stirring within her. She did her best to ignore these feelings. All they would do was complicate the situation. Multinovic was her mentor. Her instructor. And yes, her friend. That was what he would remain.

Natalia peeled away her false skin and used a towel to wipe off her makeup. She removed a curly-gray wig and let down her own hair, which was back to its natural brown and had grown below her shoulders again over the course of the winter. "I think I prefer my younger self. No need to rush things." Natalia walked into the kitchen to plug in the kettle. "Would you like some tea?" she shouted into the other room.

"Yes, please," came the reply.

Natalia took two mugs and placed them on the counter. It was mid-March and her anxiety was growing with each passing day. As the season changed from winter to spring, she knew that time was short. If Zigic was coming, it would likely be soon. Natalia had already told Raisa that she was quitting her job at the end of the week. What was the use of all of this training if she couldn't be with her family, to protect them when they needed her? She pulled a wad of Transnistrian rubles from her pocket, thumbing through the bills one at a time. It was a paltry sum for nearly five months of savings, but it was all she had. Enough for train tickets to take her family away, but what then? Where would they go? How would they eat? She felt as though the weight of the world were crushing down upon her. She shoved the rubles back into her pocket, her mind awash in despair.

Multinovic joined her in the kitchen. "Are you all right?"

"I'm fine," she said, but her voice wavering enough to give away the truth.

Multinovic looked her over with concern. "I got something special for tea today," he said. "Would you like a little treat?"

"Sure." She managed a smile.

"Sit down and close your eyes, it's a surprise."

"Ok, but that sounds awfully mysterious." Natalia took a seat at the table and clamped her eyes shut. She heard the refrigerator door open and then the rattle of plates and utensils. "What's taking you so long?!" she chided him.

"All right, you can look," he said. When Natalia opened her eyes, Multinovic sat across from her. Between them on the table was a white cake, a single candle burning on top. "Happy birthday."

"How did you know?" She was stunned.

"You told me yourself, months ago."

"I didn't think you'd remember."

"Of course I remember. Go ahead, make a wish!"

Natalia had only one thing to wish for; that she could somehow keep her family safe. She blew out the candle. Multinovic cut two pieces and put them on plates.

"You've been so good to me," said Natalia as he fetched a box of tea. "I used to be afraid of you, like everyone else. Now you're the only friend I have left."

"Oh, come on, it's just a cake!" He poured hot water into her mug.

Natalia smiled. "Thank you." She took a taste of the cake and then licked a bit of frosting from her lips.

"I know you're worried. You have a right to be."

"The snow is nearly all gone, even in the hills. It could happen any day."

"We don't know they'll come. There is a chance he's forgotten all about you."

"I know you don't believe that."

Multinovic shook his head. "You love them very much. Your family."

"They are everything to me. Not that there haven't been some rough periods. There was a time when I fought with my mother constantly." She took another bite.

"The teenage years. I think we all go through that, don't we?"

"Did you?"

"Me? Of course. You could say I was a very independent type."

"And you still are."

"Yes."

"When was the last time you saw your parents?"

"Only my mother is left...," he replied. "I've neglected her, there's no question."

"Maybe you should pay her a visit?"

"Yes, I should. Maybe someday I even will." He drank a sip of tea. "But you and your mother, you don't fight anymore?"

"No. I think my brother Leon cured me of my rebellious ways."

"Your brother?"

"Mmm, hmm. Aren't you going to eat your cake?"

Multinovic took a bite. "Not bad," he said.

"Did you bake it yourself?"

"I did."

Natalia raised both eyebrows. "You are a talented man."

"Thanks, but don't change the subject. How does Leon fit into all of this?"

"I'm surprised that you even care."

Multinovic shrugged. "Why shouldn't I?"

"I don't know," Natalia replied, but the fact that he did was a testament to how close they really had become. "I idolized my brother. When I was growing up he was everything to me," she tried to explain. "He was handsome and charming and full of life. Leon had aspirations most people in this village couldn't even comprehend. He wanted to go to college, to study literature, but you know that just isn't how things are around here. People in Drosti don't go to college. Nobody in our family ever went to college. Nobody even dreamed of it before him."

"And did he go?"

"No," Natalia shook her head. "Of course he didn't go. Olga made sure of that."

"That's his wife?"

"Yes, his wife," Natalia couldn't say it without a little bit of spite in her voice. "I shouldn't blame her, really. I know that. It wasn't her fault."

"Does it have to be anybody's fault?"

"No...," Natalia didn't seem so sure. "But when Olga came along, that's when everything changed. She was the girl who used her feminine charms to get what she wanted. Leon didn't stand a chance, and I hated her for that."

"Did he love her?"

"I don't know. He certainly fell for her. When she got pregnant the two of them weren't even married yet, but Leon did what he thought was right."

"Maybe it *was* right."

"Whether it was or not, Leon felt trapped. His first child was followed by two more, and he knew he would never get away from this life. You have to understand, Leon and I were going to leave this place together. That was always the plan. It was the secret we shared."

"Times change. Sometimes plans have to change with them."

"I don't need a lecture."

"That wasn't my intention."

"I'm sorry. I know that things change, but Leon had a hard time adjusting. As much as I like to see him as this bold, charismatic figure, he has a darker side to him. When he's happy, he's the happiest man around, and when he's not... well, I only wish I could help him."

"I'm sure you did your best."

"It wasn't enough. Leon sank deeper and deeper into the bottle until he couldn't find his way out anymore. Finally he just left. He ran off to Tiraspol. He left his wife and children behind. In Leon's mind, he thought he was doing them a favor."

"You haven't heard from him?"

"I saw him. I went to Tiraspol to find him myself. I thought I could bring him back. I thought I could save him. I even tried telling him how desperately Olga wanted him back, but he wouldn't listen." Natalia fought to mask the pain as she thought back to the days spent pleading with him to come home. "I didn't realize he was already lost. In the end I abandoned him there. I left him. Can you imagine how that feels?"

"I don't know what else you could have done."

"I ask myself that, all the time."

"He could still sort himself out, couldn't he? Maybe he just needs more time."

"I never give up hoping. Someday I'm going to come back to the house and he'll just be there, like he never left."

Multinovic gave her an encouraging nod.

"That's part of the reason I vowed to myself not to leave Drosti. So I'd be here when he finally got back."

"But you did leave."

"Yes. I did. It would be easy to blame Sonia, but the truth is I wanted to go. Those dreams I shared with Leon, they didn't die off altogether."

"So you're not really cured then, even now. You're still a rebel underneath."

Natalia picked at the remains of her cake but didn't respond.

"That's not such a bad thing," Multinovic went on. "Pledging to spend the rest of your life in this little village is a mistake. Drosti is too small to contain you. The sooner you come to terms with that, the better."

"Funny to hear that coming from you."

"My situation is different."

Natalia nodded in agreement. "I just want to take my family with me, out of harm's way. At least until this all blows over."

Multinovic put a thumb and forefinger on his chin. "Speaking of which, I have something else for you. More than just a birthday present." He reached into his shirt pocket and produced his own thick wad of bills. When he unfurled them, Natalia saw that these were not rubles. They were hundred euro notes. He spread them slightly and placed them on the table. "It's twenty-five hundred. Enough to take your family away until the fall."

"But…" Natalia was confused. "Why would you do this?"

"Take it. Please. Get your family out of here."

"I can't pay you back," she said. "Not anytime soon."

"You can survive. That is payment enough. Even if I never see you again."

Natalia looked at the money before her and then sprang to her feet, moving around the table. She squeezed Multinovic tightly and then leaned back to look him in the face. A crimson hue showed on his cheeks. "Thank you." She released her grip and took a step backwards. "I *will* try to repay you, someday. A bit at a time."

"Don't consider it a burden."

Natalia picked the notes up and shoved them into a pocket. "I'd better go."

"Yes," he agreed. "The faster you leave Drosti the better."

Natalia hurried to the door, letting herself out through the foyer and onto the street. It was a beautiful spring day with just a slight chill in the air. For the first time in as long as she could remember, Natalia was overcome with a sense of hope.

Chapter Twenty-Eight

Ivanka crossed her arms and frowned, sullenly staring at the Euro notes resting on the kitchen table. "And what did you have to do for it?"

"Nothing, mother," Natalia replied.

"Don't lie to me! I know what people are saying."

"He's a good man, mother. Don't listen to those small-minded people."

"Nobody gives away this much money without expecting something in return."

"I'm telling you, he's trying to help us, that's all!" Natalia was becoming angry. Why couldn't her mother accept that this was an offer of goodwill and nothing more? Why must there always be an ulterior motive?

Victor stood with his arms crossed, equally dubious. "Even if what you say is true, do you know what you are asking? Who will tend our fields? Feed our animals? How will we make a living when this money runs out?"

"None of that will matter if we're dead!" Natalia shot back.

"Natalia!" her mother recoiled. "Have you lost your mind? You can't believe these stories you're telling!? Not really!"

"Where would we even go?" added Victor.

"Anywhere you want," answered Natalia, though she knew their options were limited. Nobody in the family had a passport. "Tiraspol if you'd like, or even Chisinau."

"No, no, no!" Ivanka slammed her hands down on the kitchen table. "This is our home! We are not leaving! I won't hear anything more about it!"

"Mother, they will kill you if you stay! You have to believe me!"

"Nobody is coming here, Natalia! Nobody!"

"And what of the children?! Will you risk their lives as well? I won't let you do that!"

"Please, Natalia! I know that you saw some horrible things, but you must forget about these men. It is time to move on."

"I wish I could forget, mother. If only I could. But Goran Zigic won't let me forget. He made sure of that." Natalia unbuttoned her pants and yanked them down to her thighs in one violent motion and then pulled up her shirt with one hand. With the fingers of her other she traced the scar, carved in the letter Z. She showed off the cigarette burns across her stomach and down the insides of her legs. "No, I never will forget."

Ivanka took a step closer. "He did this to you?" She was aghast, seeing this evidence of her daughter's torture.

"It was nothing compared to what he did to Sonia."

Ivanka looked away, covering her mouth, yet still not willing to believe. Not willing to admit that someone would do this to her beautiful daughter.

"We can send you and your sister away, with Olga and the children," said Victor, succumbing to reality more quickly than his wife.

"No!" Natalia was emphatic. "We all go!"

"I must take care of the animals," Victor protested.

"Vladimir can watch the animals. At his own farm. We can sell them. Whatever he'll give us!"

Victor turned to Ivanka for her reaction.

"If we went to Tiraspol, perhaps we could see Leon," she said.

"Yes!" Natalia replied. Any excuse that might help convince them to leave was a good one. "The children *should* spend time with their father. But we must go quickly. These men could come at any time."

"How quickly?" asked Victor.

"Tonight. We will go to the hotel in town and then board a bus first thing in the morning."

"So soon?" Ivanka was distraught.

"The sooner the better. I'll tell the others to start packing." Natalia moved out of the room to gather the rest of the family.

Chapter Twenty-Nine

It took three trips in the battered Lada to get everyone into town. Twice the car became stuck in the mud, and Natalia and Rita were covered in brown muck by the time they'd pushed it out. To Rita it was all a grand adventure but Natalia was on edge, expecting Zigic's men to appear at any moment. Even when the family was safely checked into the hotel, she worried that the men might show up looking for a room. They had to stay someplace when they came to town, after all. The proprietor, an old family friend, assured Natalia that she would admit no other guests.

"If you see any other foreigners at all I want you to let us know immediately," Natalia said.

"Yes," the proprietor assured her. "Don't worry about a thing."

Natalia nodded. Most likely she would worry for the rest of her life, but getting out of Drosti would help. When she had showered and changed into clean clothes, Natalia stepped out, leaving her family in the hotel with strict instructions to stay put until she returned. She wanted to see Gregor one last time, to thank him for everything he had done. The training, the money…the friendship. Or was it more than that? A sense of melancholy haunted her, knowing that she very well may never see him again. There was so much she wished she could say. So much she wanted him to understand. So much she didn't understand herself. The emotions she was feeling had crept up on her over time. She'd gone from fearing him, to pitying him, to feeling an unlikely connection; two outcasts against the world. The thought of not having him in her life filled Natalia with dread and sorrow. He was a war criminal in hiding, despite his protestations of innocence. An arms dealer, more than twice her age. But the feelings didn't lie and she was almost certain he had them, too.

Natalia walked briskly through the village, pistol tucked into her waistband in the small of her back. She was on constant alert, so close to being away safely. One more night in the village and they'd be gone. When she rang the bell, Multinovic buzzed her into the foyer and then opened the inner door. "Is everything all right?"

"Yes. They're at the hotel. We'll leave town in the morning."

"Wonderful." He showed his own sign of relief. "I am very glad to hear it."

"I just wanted to thank you again. You don't know what this means to me. Not just the money, but everything. You've taught me so much..."

"I hope it is enough," Multinovic answered.

"It will have to be."

"I just wish I could have left you as you were; that innocent young girl I used to see in the restaurant, with the light in her eyes."

"You didn't steal my innocence. You've just made me a survivor."

"You've always been that, whether you realize it or not." Multinovic stepped aside from the doorway. "Would you care to come in? I'd like to give you one more lesson, if it's not too late. In fact, I was hoping you'd come by."

"What kind of lesson?"

"Follow me and I'll show you, but promise you won't take it the wrong way. It's just another part of your training."

"Something new then?" She was slightly suspicious.

"Yes. Something new." Multinovic led her into the next room where two place settings rested on the table, an unlit candle between them. Draped across a chair was a short red dress. On the floor, a set of matching red shoes with stiletto heels.

"What is this?" The whole setup made her uneasy.

"I want to impart to you some sophistication. I know the source is dubious, but you walk like a farm girl. You eat like a farm girl. You carry yourself like a farm girl. It is charming in its own way, but there are times when you may have to pass yourself off as a woman with breeding. I know that one evening is not enough, but if you don't mind, I think we should try."

Natalia lifted the dress from the chair, thinking back to the last time she was made to put on such feminine clothing.

"If you'd prefer not to…" Multinovic started, sensing her unease.

"No. I'd love to." She picked up the shoes and moved into his office, closing the door behind her. A few minutes later she emerged with the skin-tight dress clinging to every curve, suddenly self-conscious when she saw the look in Multinovic's eyes. "What do you think?" she asked, just to hear him say it.

"Impressive." He tried to maintain a businesslike air. "Let's get to work. Try walking across the room, stop, turn and come back." Natalia followed his directions but had barely taken a step when Multinovic began calling out, "Chin up, and let me see some sway in those hips! Remember, you're a woman, not a farmhand!"

Natalia couldn't help but laugh. "Who are you to judge?!"

"I did tell you the source was dubious, but I am a man, after all. I've been watching women all my life."

"Fine then, I'll humor you," Natalia replied, but with each pass she felt a little less awkward. "I think the martial arts training was easier!" she joked as she went.

"Just remember, to look alluring you must feel alluring, in every fiber of your soul. You must exude self-confidence!"

Natalia recognized the irony in that last statement. The man who implored her to be confident was the same man who made her feel flustered. She wanted to follow his advice. She wanted to be alluring. For him. She closed her eyes as she went. During all of her time as a captive, she'd willed herself to be as unattractive as possible, hoping those men might choose someone else. Now with Gregor as her audience, she let her body move, swaying with the rhythm of desire. She opened her eyes and turned, walking up and back three times, a woman in charge.

Multinovic coughed lightly. "That's very good. "I think we can move on."

"Are you sure?"

"Yes." He looked away, cheeks lightly flushed. "Why don't we go over table manners next?"

"What's wrong?" Natalia laughed, sensing the power she held in this dress, these shoes. A power she'd never fully harnessed before, yet intuitively always knew she had. It was a power that he was trying to fend off, apparently with less success than he wished.

"Nothing is wrong," he coughed again. Moving into his kitchen he lifted the lid off a skillet to reveal two boneless breasts of chicken, simmering in a cream sauce. In another pot, red potatoes were at a low boil. He opened his refrigerator and took out a Caesar salad and a bottle of wine.

"How did you know I would come by tonight?" Natalia asked.

"I merely hoped. It would have been a shame to eat all of this by myself. I'm not keeping you from anything, am I? It is your birthday after all."

"No, my parents forgot all about it. Only my sister remembered, but I told her to keep quiet. They've got enough on their minds."

"All right." He placed the salad on the counter and then opened the wine and poured two glasses. Lastly, he took a match and lit the single candle in the center of the table.

"Is this our first date?" Natalia asked with a coy tilt of the head.

"And I'm afraid our last," he answered. "I'm not ashamed to say, I'll be very sad to see you go. I've appreciated your company these last few months."

"Why not come with us?" Natalia tried to downplay her eagerness. "This is no life for you here, all alone. You know it's true. Once I'm gone you'll be right back to how you were before, with nobody to talk to at all. I don't see how you can stand it!"

Multinovic used a spatula to lift the chicken onto two plates, adding potatoes to each and then some salad before placing them on the table. "So you think I should go on the run, with the entire Nicolaev family?" He laughed at this prospect. "Somehow I don't think I could stand that any better."

"Oh, you know, we're not so bad. Despite what I might have said."

"I don't suppose I'd be made to babysit, would I?"

"Ok, fine! Don't come! But at least know you'd be welcome, any time."

"Thank you," he said with sincerity. "I do know."

They took their seats facing each other, the flame from the candle between them casting a warm, flickering glow across his well-worn features. He raised his glass for a toast. "To life," he said. "That most precious commodity."

"And friendship." She raised her own. "That makes it worth living."

Multinovic touched his glass to hers.

"What will you teach me now?"

"I don't know," he answered. "Perhaps I just wanted one last dinner together."

Natalia offered a smile. "You could have just asked." She cut a piece of her chicken and took a taste. The sauce was nothing she'd tried before. Creamy but with a hint of pepper, mustard, perhaps tarragon... "You keep surprising me."

"Thank you."

"Where did you learn to cook?"

"From my mother."

"Your mother?" Natalia seemed surprised.

"Why not? Can't a boy learn to cook from his mother?"

"For some reason it's hard to believe you really even have one. It seems more likely that you just appeared on this planet out of thin air."

"No, I do have a mother. And I was young once, too. I know that's probably hard to believe as well."

"I'd like to have seen it. I'll bet you were a real hell-raiser."

"You have me all figured out, don't you?" He laughed lightly.

"Not quite," she said. "But I'd like to."

When they'd finished dinner, Multinovic rose from his seat and carried the plates to the kitchen. "There's still some cake left if you'd like it." He looked back at her. "Though I suspect you'll be wanting to return to your family."

"I'm not in a huge hurry," Natalia replied. Of course he was right. She should get back to the hotel, yet she was loathe to go. She yearned to stay with him for as long as she could. This swell of emotion caught her off guard, but there was no denying it. Natalia lifted the empty wine glasses from the table and moved close, leaning around him to place them in the sink. They faced one another, their bodies inches apart, held in place by an unmistakable magnetism that made the hairs on her forearm stand on end. "It's a shame you didn't teach me to dance," she said quietly. When he didn't move away, Natalia placed her hands on either side of his waist and stared into his eyes for a few long seconds.

"I never was much of a dancer." Multinovic was frozen in place.

"I doubt that." Natalia slid her arms around his back and leaned close. She'd tried to fight it, for months she'd been trying, but that battle was lost.

"You don't have to do this," he said. "You don't owe me anything."

"Is that what you think this is?"

"I don't know what to think."

"Then don't," she answered. "Don't think at all."

She felt his hands on her hips and knew there was no turning back. He closed his eyes and their lips came together, brushing softly as his strong arms embraced her. She'd wanted this for so long, and now Natalia simply let go, losing herself to the swirling emotions of desire.

Chapter Thirty

The sun was already up when Natalia awoke with Multinovic's arm draped over her. The bliss was hard to shake, but she looked to the clock on his bedside table. It was six-thirty. As much as she wanted to stay forever in his embrace, she knew that she had to get back to the hotel. She never should have stayed away from her family for so long. Sliding out from under the covers, she moved across the room. Multinovic opened his eyes and watched her naked body in the morning light, for the first and likely the last time.

"Good morning," he said.

"Did I wake you? I'm sorry that I have to leave so early." She paused in the bathroom doorway. She liked being naked in front of him. It felt natural. She liked the way he seemed to appreciate it, taking her in from head to toe, his gaze pausing on her every curve. It was enough to leave her just a little bit heartbroken that this beginning also had to be an end. Was it better to have come so late than to not have come at all? She didn't have time to contemplate such questions. Today was too important a day to be distracted.

Natalia turned and moved into the bathroom. She showered quickly and then toweled herself off before retrieving her old clothes from the office. When she was dressed, she tucked her gun back into her waistband and laced up her shoes. In the kitchen she met Multinovic, who stood in his pajama pants holding the red dress and stiletto heels in a plastic bag. "Don't forget these. They're a gift, you know."

"I couldn't. You've done so much already."

"Believe me, I'm not going to wear them."

Natalia laughed and then took the bag from his hands. "Thank you, then. Though I don't know when I'll have the chance to ever wear them again."

"You never know," he said. "Care for some coffee?"

"No, I'd better get going."

"Yes. Yes, I understand…"

They stood facing one another, the bittersweet aftermath of their night together hanging between them. Multinovic leaned forward to kiss her on the nose. "You know how much I care for you. Nothing is ever going to change that."

Natalia grabbed him around the small of his back and pulled him close. "If you're worried that last night might come between us somehow, don't. There's really no point."

"No, I suppose not." He took her in his arms.

Natalia planted her lips against his in a long, last passionate kiss. When she finally came up for air they held each other for a few moments more, her head against his shoulder. "I really do need to go," she said finally before releasing her grasp.

"Good luck."

"Good bye. Thank you for everything." She hurried through the door to the foyer, looking back one last time to see him watching with sad eyes. The door closed behind her and she moved through the next, on out to the street.

Outside, the air was brisk and the ground covered with a thin crust of frost. Her shoes made a crunching sound as she walked up the sidewalk, past the other abandoned warehouses and on toward the center of town. On the main road through the village Natalia saw a fresh set of tire tracks. They were large and wide. The tires knobby and new. Nobody in Drosti had a car like that. She picked up her pace. Her fears swelled when she didn't see the family's Lada parked in front of the hotel. She rang the bell long and hard.

The proprietor opened the door and Natalia moved inside to find her mother having breakfast in the kitchen. "Nice of you to join us." A smug Ivanka waved a piece of toast in Natalia's direction.

"Where is the car?!" Natalia replied.

"You might as well eat." Ivanka nodded toward the bread and jam on the table.

"Please, mother, where is the car?" Natalia pleaded.

"Your father went to the farm with Vladimir, to take care of the animals."

"No!" Natalia raised her voice. "I told him not to go back there!"

"He took the gun. Don't worry, they'll be back soon."

"Who else went with him?"

"Rita went to help. And Constantine. Somebody had to go! And you, off with this man…"

A surge of panic rose within Natalia. Those tracks could be from any number of sources, she told herself. Maybe a government minister passing through the village, or someone else on the way to Tiraspol. Yet no matter how hard she tried, Natalia couldn't shake the feeling of terror. "You stay here! I'm going to get them!" Before Ivanka could answer, Natalia rushed back out into the street. This time she ran as fast as she could. At Multinovic's place, she rang the bell twice and then pounded on the door. He appeared in an instant, swinging it wide. "What is it?"

"I saw some tracks. Maybe it is nothing, but my father's gone back to the farm."

"What type of tracks?"

"New tires. Big and wide. Nothing I've seen before."

"Come with me." He led her inside, wasting no time in throwing on his clothes and boots and then arming himself.

"I shouldn't have left them alone last night. I never should have stayed over here." Natalia was weighed down by guilt.

"Don't blame yourself. It won't do you any good."
"I know, but…"
"I mean it! This is not the time to be emotional."

Natalia nodded. He was right, of course. He was always right. She followed him to his garage at the back where Multinovic moved between a small white delivery truck and a sleek grey motorcycle to open a large door facing the alley. He took two helmets from the wall, handing one to Natalia before he hopped onto the bike and started it up. Multinovic rode through the door and Natalia closed it behind them. She climbed on the back of the bike and held him tightly around the waist as they sped off toward the farm.

By the time they joined the main road the tracks had melted away but Natalia felt Multinovic pull back on the throttle and they hurtled down the highway. At the turnoff to the farm, the tracks reappeared, this time in a thin layer of mud. They doubled up on the dirt road and then continued south. Had the vehicle come and gone? The motorcycle bounced along the rutted road, through pockets of melting snow. When they crested the hill above the farm, Multinovic came to a quick stop. The tire tracks continued down toward the house, but the only car visible was the Lada. Beside it lay a body, face down. Even from this distance Natalia knew it was her father. She leapt off the bike and began to run, her mind in a daze. "Papa!" Natalia screamed, pulling off her helmet and throwing it aside. Time stood still as her legs moved one in front of the other, independent of thought; she heard nothing, saw nothing, only her father, still motionless before her. When she reached him, Natalia rolled him onto his back and wiped the mud from his face, desperate to clear his airway. His eyes were wide and unresponsive. His chest was red with blood. "Father, oh father…" She clutched his lifeless body and heaved with sobs.

Behind her, Multinovic pulled up on his motorcycle and then dropped it to the ground before brandished his own pistol. "Who is that in the car?"

Natalia lifted her head. "The car?" she repeated his words. "Rita!" She leapt to her feet. "Constantine?!" Slumped in the Lada's passenger seat was Vladimir, a bullet wound to the head. The backseat was empty. "Rita!" Natalia shouted again as she ran toward the house.

"Wait!" Multinovic hollered after her. "Be careful!"

Natalia paid him no heed. She rushed into the house and darted from room to room. "Rita! Constantine! Where are you?!"

Multinovic bounded in behind her, gun in the air. A mysterious whimper came from somewhere inside the wall and he spun around to face it.

"No! Wait!" Natalia darted in front of him. She pushed on the panel to reveal the crawl space hidden within. Huddled inside was Constantine, arms around his knees, struggling to breathe. "Oh, Constantine! I'm here!" Natalia cried, reaching inside to pick the boy up. She carried him into the living room and placed him on the couch. His face was pale white as his lungs fought for oxygen.

"What's wrong with him?" said Multinovic.

"Asthma!" She dug in his pocket and retrieved an inhaler before propping him up and holding it to his mouth. "Here, Constantine. Here is your medicine!" She pressed down on the top and he sucked in his dose, gasping as his passages began to clear. "That's it, just breathe," she said as the color returned to his cheeks. His eyes were wide with fear as he looked from Natalia to Multinovic and back.

"He's in shock," said Multinovic.

Natalia leaned closer to her nephew. "You're safe now Constantine, but you must tell us. It is very important. Where is Rita?"

Constantine's mouth opened and closed a few times without making a sound. "Gone," he finally managed. "Gone away."

"Gone where?" Natalia fought to contain her fears, trying to push aside the knowledge that her father was outside on his back, in the mud, dead. "Where did she go?"

"The bad men took her," Constantine answered.

Natalia looked up to Multinovic. "I'm going after her," she said.

"I'll go," Multinovic replied.

"No! Please. Watch my nephew." She eased Constantine backwards on the couch. "Don't let him see my father."

"Natalia..." he didn't know how to argue with her.

"Please, just do as I ask."

"They're heading south," Multinovic conceded. "They won't be expecting you. That's your only advantage."

"They came all this way. How could they have left without me?"

"Zigic could have sent anyone. Men who never saw you before. They probably think they have you."

Natalia wasted no more time on conjecture. She ran out the door and across the yard past her father, reaching down to grab her helmet and slide it on her head. Next she lifted the bike from the mud, climbed on and hit the starter, revving the engine twice.

"Wait!" Multinovic called after her from the doorway. "The bike, it's low on fuel! Do you have any extra stored here?"

"There's no time!" Natalia popped the bike into gear and then raced off down the muddy road. At the highway she turned left, following the tire tracks south and scanning the horizon for any signs of a vehicle. She could feel the pressure of the gun against her back as she ducked into the wind and flew along the asphalt at full speed. If only she could catch them…

After half an hour, Natalia finally spotted her quarry in the distance. It was a large black SUV, passing over a knoll about half a kilometer ahead. Natalia crouched low, trying to coax every bit of velocity that she could from her machine. She was gaining. The car grew in size until it was just a few hundred meters away. Natalia knew she couldn't shoot the driver. Likewise for shooting out the tires. If they crashed at high speed, Rita might not survive. Natalia would have to wait until they slowed down, passing through the next village. But would the driver notice her trailing behind them in the meantime?

Natalia matched their speed and kept her distance at roughly 150 meters. The next village was only ten kilometers away. If they slowed enough, she could pull up right alongside and shoot the tires, then the driver. Or should she pass them now and set up an ambush? Block the road up ahead and make them come to a stop? She liked this second option better. She'd lay her bike down in the road if she had to. Perhaps even lie down beside it, faking an accident. When they slowed to take a look she'd come up firing. She pulled back on the throttle, gaining on them once again. As she drew close, Natalia saw the outline of her sister sitting in the back seat. Two men sat in the front. "Hold on, Rita, I'm coming!" she thought to herself. But then the bike began to sputter. It shook and coughed. "No, no, no!" Natalia shouted out loud this time but it was no use. The engine cut out altogether. Her speed ebbed away and Natalia coasted to the shoulder. She turned the key in desperation, pressing repeatedly on the starter but to no effect. She looked to the fuel gauge. Empty. Up ahead the SUV went over another low hill and disappeared. Natalia tore off her helmet and heaved it down the highway, shaking with helplessness and rage. With each passing second her lovely, innocent little sister was slipping farther from her grasp, on into that dark hell of an existence Natalia knew so well.

Chapter Thirty-One

Multinovic let the smoke from his cigarette swirl inside his lungs as he paced back and forth inside his courtyard. "I can't go with you," he exhaled, dropping the butt to the floor and stubbing it out with a heel. "You have to understand, in my business, if the Turkish government got hold of me…"

"I'm not asking you to go," said Natalia.

Multinovic paused, crossing his arms. "I can handle the logistics. Supplies, transportation…"

"Whatever you can manage. But don't feel obliged."

"I won't let you go unprepared. Come, let's see what we can do." Multinovic led her into the elevator, closed the door and pushed the down button. When they emerged in his underground storeroom he took out a large black duffel, unzipped it and threw it down on a work bench. He went from one crate to another, pulling out a compact machine gun and grenade launcher from one and plastic explosives from another, tossing them all in the bag. Ammunition clips, grenades and a makeup kit. He held up a bulletproof vest in front of Natalia to check the size before tossing it in as well. When he was finished, Multinovic zipped up the duffel and lifted it to gauge the weight. The heavy-duty canvas strained from the contents, but it would hold. He handed the bag to Natalia. "Just realize what you're up against. I honestly don't expect you to survive."

"Thank you for the vote of confidence." Natalia felt the heft of the bag, keenly aware of the enormity of her task. She was returning all alone to those menacing streets, to take on an entire criminal network, yet she couldn't allow herself to contemplate the odds. Any hope of success meant that she had to maintain her focus. She had to believe it could be done. "When do we go?"

"Tonight. I'll have everything arranged. Go, be with your family. Meet me back here at dusk."

It wasn't really a road they followed. It was more a series of primitive tracks, across farmlands and over rolling hills. Natalia wondered how many times he'd navigated this route on his own, eluding the border police. His truck's lights were off, but Multinovic drove using night-vision goggles, amplifying the pale light of the moon to show the way. When they hit a particularly large bump, Natalia braced herself against the door handle.

"Sorry about that one, I'll try to warn you next time," said Multinovic.

"It's all right." The physical sensation of the journey was a distraction from her true concerns. Since they set off several hours earlier she'd been preoccupied with thoughts of Rita, playing through her mind what her sister must be going through and what she had in store if Natalia failed her. She thought of her father, who she'd failed already. And she thought about killing another man herself. Goran Zigic had to die. That much she knew. When she'd killed Dusan it was without any thought at all, merely instinct. Now she faced the prospect of hunting a man down by design. Killing him in cold blood. If anyone in the world deserved to die, it was Zigic. Natalia's heart yearned for vengeance, for Sonia, for her father, for every evil thing Zigic had ever done to her or anyone else, but this was about even more than that. With Zigic alive, Natalia would never have a moment of peace in her life, always wondering when he might next come for her. Killing him was the only way. Whatever moral implications there were to taking another human life, she had to put them aside. This was a task that she needed to accomplish, for her own survival and the survival of her family. "How far will you take me?" she asked Multinovic.

"Bulgaria. A man will be waiting with a boat. He's done the run many times. You'll be safe with him. He will take you to the Turkish coast."

"And then?"

"You'll be driven into the city. After that, you're on your own. Find an out-of-the-way hotel, settle in and do your homework. Don't be too hasty. That's the best way to wind up dead. If you think that you know where she is, you have to observe the place. Make sure you know how many guards there are. Try to determine where they are posted, where your sister is being held, how to get in and how to get out."

"I know the layout already. I lived there."

"Things change. She might not be in the same house that you were. Just be careful."

"I'll try." Natalia hoped she'd have the patience to heed his advice.

"He is a coward, you know. The biggest coward I ever met. I don't think I mentioned that before."

"Who Zigic?! I don't think so. Maybe he changed since you knew him."

"No, it's true. He acts like a tough guy, abusing the weak and the powerless, but put him in danger and you'll see the real Goran Zigic. You'll see the Goran Zigic who cowers in fear like a child. Worse than a child."

"I find that hard to imagine."

"You haven't seen him under fire, with tears streaming down his face, snot running from his nose. You haven't seen him pissing in his pants."

Natalia tried to picture it. "I haven't seen that, no, but I think I'd like to."

"Just realize, his cowardice makes him unpredictable, and that makes him even more dangerous."

"If you're worried that I might underestimate him, don't. I know exactly what he's capable of." Natalia leaned back against the headrest, thinking of Zigic lying in a foxhole, pissing in his pants. The image gave her a small measure of strength. In the back of her mind, she'd always thought of him as invincible. She didn't see him that way anymore. The man she was going up against had a weakness. If at all possible, she would find a way to exploit it.

By dawn they were back on a paved highway, driving through Romania on the way toward Bucharest. "You should get some rest," Multinovic said. "Go in the back if you'd like, I have a blanket there. You can make some space and lie down."

"Yes, I am very tired." Natalia disappeared into the back of the truck but returned a moment later with the blanket, curling up beneath it on the passenger seat and closing her eyes. She kept them closed for several minutes, but she couldn't keep the disturbing images from flashing through her mind. Zigic carving her open with his knife. Dusan writhing on the ground. Rita disappearing over the horizon in a black SUV. Her father's blood-soaked body. Natalia's eyes sprang open. She pulled the blanket up and over her shoulders, trying to think back to better times. She saw her father as a young man, chasing his daughters around the village square, always letting them stay one step ahead. It was a rare playful moment for him, but one that stayed with Natalia. She would carry it with her always, deep inside her heart. "Do you mind if we listen to some music?" she asked.

"You can try the radio."

Natalia pressed the power switch and then scanned through the dial, passing some news reports in Romanian that she couldn't understand and a heavy metal rock station before finally stopping on the sad strains of a solo violin. "Is this all right?"

"Fine."

Resting on a console between them was a pack of cigarettes. Perhaps they might calm her nerves. She lifted the pack and then pressed in the knob on the truck's lighter. "Would you like one?" she asked.

"Sure."

When the knob popped out she lit two cigarettes with the glowing coil and handed one across. "Why do you sell weapons to terrorists?" It was a question that had bothered her for months but she'd been afraid to ask.

"How do you know they're terrorists?"

"Aren't they?"

"One could argue that the PKK are simply fighting for their liberation. You could say they are patriots."

"The PKK?"

"Kurdish separatists."

"I see. And what of your other customers?"

Multinovic took a long draw on his cigarette, his silence demonstrating his displeasure. "War is a dirty business. I'm the first to admit it, but sometimes people deserve the chance to fight back. You're the perfect example of that, are you not?"

"But what about Ukraine? You told me yourself that you sell to both sides there. How can you do that? How can you profit while these slaughter one another?"

"None of this seemed to bother you before." He was obviously perturbed.

"I just want to understand."

"Remember, I didn't choose this life. It was forced upon me by circumstance."

"Everyone has choices in life. I'm sure there are plenty of other things you could do."

Multinovic looked at her sidelong.

"Forget it," she said. "Forget I even mentioned it."

They drove in silence for a while before he spoke again. "You're right, everyone has choices," he admitted. "Mine haven't always been the best."

"So why don't you make a change? It's not too late."

"I am trying."

"What do you mean trying?"

"I haven't had a new shipment in months. Maybe you noticed, the crates in my place slowly disappearing. A going-out-of-business sale you might say."

It struck Natalia that without the business he would no longer have any reason to stay in Drosti. No reason at all. That realization left her unexpectedly wistful. "What will you do next?"

"I hadn't worked that out exactly. I owe a visit to my mother. Beyond that… time will tell."

"When will you go?"

"Soon."

"Were you going to tell me?"

Multinovic took his time in answering. "I was hoping I wouldn't have to. I thought you'd be the one leaving first."

"Why would you think that?"

"Because, there's no future for you in Drosti. You deserve so much more."

"I could say the same about you."

"At least I've come to accept it. I'll be honest, you're the one who made it obvious how pathetic my life had become."

"Ha!" Natalia laughed. "Somebody had to." From the dim light of the dash, she could just make out a smile cross his lips. She took a last puff on her cigarette and then cracked her window to flick it out. She closed her eyes again, this time concentrating on the sounds of the music. Natalia would miss Multinovic when he left, if she made it back alive herself. She felt as though they were partners, so comfortable with one another that she could tell him anything and ask anything in return. He made her feel safe, and never so much as when he'd held her in his arms. What they'd shared would always be with her and that would have to be enough. At this point, however, her future didn't matter. Neither did her past. All that mattered was bringing Rita home.

After some minutes, a heaviness began to overtake Natalia. When she opened her eyes again, it was unclear how much time had passed. The early light of dawn lit up the eastern sky as they drove through a quiet rural town not unlike her own. "How long was I asleep?"

"A few hours. We'll stop here for a short break. We need to eat."

"I can drive."

"After we eat." Multinovic pulled up to a small, non-descript restaurant and parked the truck around the back. They entered through the rear and Multinovic chose a table by the door. Two older men with bushy gray moustaches eyed them from another table in the center of the room. Multinovic pretended not to notice, but Natalia knew he saw everything. He never missed a detail, but he also did his best not to draw undue attention to himself. In a town so small, this was impossible, Natalia knew from experience.

A round woman in her late 50's ambled to their table with menus in her hand. "It's been some time." She placed the menus on the table.

"Two eggs, sausage, bread," Multinovic said briskly, "and a coffee."

"The same for me, please," said Natalia.

"You'd like your bread toasted?" the woman asked.

"Yes, please," said Natalia.

The waitress picked up her menus and walked into the kitchen.

"You told me not to follow patterns. Always vary your routine, you said."

"Do as I say, not as I do. This place is as far as I can drive without a break and besides, there aren't a lot of options around here." The waitress reappeared with two cups of coffee on a tray. She placed them on the table with a bowl of sugar and a small container of milk.

Natalia looked around the restaurant at the faded, peeling paint and the grime worn into the tables and chairs. After a short wait, the waitress brought out two plates of sausage and eggs along with a basket of toast, some butter and jam. Multinovic wasted no time digging into his food. Natalia cut a slice of sausage and blew on it twice before easing it into her mouth. It was only when she'd tasted it that she realized how hungry she really was. It was her first real meal in a day and a half.

By nightfall they were back on another ancient dirt track, with Multinovic behind the wheel again in his night-vision goggles. He flipped them up long enough to check their position on his GPS. "Welcome to Bulgaria," he said.

"How much farther do we have to go?"

"We meet the boat at midnight. Three hours more and I'll be rid of you," he tried to make light of it.

"You know you'll miss me." She didn't admit that her stomach was tied in knots. Three more hours. After that, the decisions would be all hers. The smallest miscalculation could be catastrophic, but she couldn't dwell on that. She had to believe in herself to succeed. Natalia just wished she could let Rita know that help was on the way…

As midnight approached, Natalia felt like that small child she'd been so long ago, on the way to school and about to be dropped off into the unknown for the very first time. Multinovic was her friend, her mentor, her protector. She was loathe to leave him behind. When he finally pulled over they were on a small rise overlooking the sea. "This is it." He checked his watch. "We're a few minutes late."

"Is that a problem?"

"I hope not." He hopped out of the truck and walked around to the back. Natalia met him as he opened the rear door. She unzipped her bag and took out her full-length grey overcoat, putting it on to repel a damp, cold breeze coming off the water. Feeling around inside the bag she found her dark Russian hat and put that on as well, pulling the flaps down over her ears.

"What if the boat is gone?" she asked.

Multinovic picked up the bag and closed the door. "Follow me. We'll find out." He led her down a dirt path in the moonlight, through a grass field and then a small clump of trees before they emerged in a small cove. On the far side, shaded from the moonlight by a low cliff, Natalia thought she could make out a shape on the sand, though it could easily have been a large rock. They moved across the beach and Multinovic gave a low whistle in two bursts. He was greeted by three bursts in return. As they drew closer, Natalia saw that the shape was a black inflatable boat resting at the water's edge. Standing beside the craft was a stocky man in dark all-weather gear with a pair of night-vision binoculars in one hand.

"Gregor!" The man greeted Multinovic with a bear hug. "I was beginning to think your luck had run out."

"Never," Multinovic answered. "Natalia, meet Luca."

"So this is your cargo?" Luca sized up Natalia. In return, she tried to get a read on the man, but in the dark it was nearly impossible. She could tell that he had dark curly hair and a trim beard. His demeanor seemed lighter than she'd expected for a man of his profession. He had an energy about him suggesting that he enjoyed his line of work, as though it were all a grand adventure.

"I've got a few other things for Vadim. Come, give me a hand," Multinovic said to Luca. "Natalia, you stay here with the boat."

She waited alone on the beach while the two men went to the truck. All was quiet but for the sound of a few small waves washing up and down the sand. Natalia pulled her coat around herself tightly in an attempt to stay warm. Riding in this open boat, she realized, was not going to be easy. After a few minutes, the men returned with a crate and loaded it aboard. Natalia placed her duffel bag on top. When everything was lashed down, the three of them pushed the boat backwards into the sea. Luca hopped on board first and lowered dual props into the water. "Come on!" he called to her and then fired up the engines. Natalia climbed aboard as the props caught and the boat backed away from the beach. Luca spun the craft around and then dropped both gears to forward, gunning the throttle. Natalia held on tightly, watching Multinovic's figure as he hurried along the shore. Before he disappeared into the brush she saw him stop and look up, raising a hand to wave farewell. She wondered if she would ever see him again.

Chapter Thirty-Two

Natalia held tightly to a line along the gunwale as they bounced across a churning sea, saltwater spraying over the bow into her face and soaking her coat and pants and hat. She ducked her head low into the wind. Beneath her, stretching the length of the boat, were tightly-packed burlap bags. Whatever was inside them, Natalia knew that if they were caught by the authorities she wouldn't see daylight for a very long time. Her life was in the hands of this man she'd never before met and who she could barely even see in the darkness. All Natalia could do was hold on and hope for the best. "How long will the crossing take?" she shouted over the roar of the engines.

"Three hours!" Luca shouted back. "If we have no problems!" He reached under the steering console and pulled out a plastic tarp, tossing it to her. The wind tried to tear the tarp from her hands as Natalia unfolded it, but she managed to wrap it around her body, providing some extra protection. She scanned the horizon. It was only darkness but for the lights of one ship churning northwards in the distance. "Oil tanker!" Luca yelled. "Not a problem! It is only the small boats we worry about, but even then they'll never catch us! We're too fast for them!" Natalia could just make out his grin; a row of white teeth gleaming in the moonlight. She wrapped the tarp more snugly around herself and curled up on the heaving bundles beneath.

By the time he eased back on the throttle several hours later, Natalia was completely numb below the waist, her legs cramped and tingling, her entire body shivering from the cold and wet. As the craft slowed, she saw the dark outline of a rocky coast just ahead. Luca pulled out a small light and flashed it three times. A return signal came back from the shore and he held his night-vision binoculars to his face.

"This entry is a little tricky. I suggest you hold on." Luca gunned the throttles, sending the boat straight toward a low rock shelf. At the last possible moment he raised the props from the water and Natalia bounced into the air as the boat went up and over, coming to rest in a shallow, protected pool. Three men emerged from the shadows, wading toward them through thigh-deep water. Luca shut off his engines and jumped out to meet them. He grasped the hand of one man briefly before all four went to work unloading the cargo and carrying it ashore.

Natalia unlashed her own bag and took it by the handles. She lowered herself over the edge of the inflatable into the frigid water, hoisted the heavy duffel on one shoulder and trudged toward dry land. When she'd climbed onto the rocky shore, she dropped her bag at her feet and watched the men work, carrying in the crate and then one bag after another until they were finished.

"End of the line!" Luca said to Natalia as they set the last bag down beside her.

"But, where am I?" she asked.

"They will take you from here." Luca nodded toward the others before wading through the water and hopping back into his boat. The three men helped push the craft backwards over the outcropping and into the sea. When he was clear of the rocks, Luca started up his engines again and just as quickly as they'd arrived, he was off.

The others paid Natalia little attention, though she couldn't help but feel uneasy, here in the dark on a deserted shoreline with three nefarious strangers. She reached into her bag and retrieved her pistol, tucking it into her waist. Two of the men continued hauling the bags up a small hill while the third pulled out a cigarette and lighter. Natalia saw his rough, unshaven face in the yellow flicker of flame. He pocketed the lighter and turned toward her in the darkness, the red tip of his cigarette glowing as he inhaled. "Sigara?" He held out the pack.

"No," she replied. "Thank you." She followed him up the hill and over to the other side, where the two others were loading the cargo into an old van. There were no other signs of life in any direction. She hoped this was Turkey at least, though she could not even be sure of that.

When the last of the contraband was loaded, Natalia put her duffel inside the van and then climbed in after, taking a seat on the floor. The men sat three across a bench seat in front. No words were spoken as they drove off, bouncing across yet another rough dirt road. Before long they hit a paved highway and when the ride smoothed out, Natalia took off her hat and slid out of her wet jacket and shirt, placing the pistol beside her. She unzipped the duffel and felt inside with one hand until she found a mostly dry shirt and a sweater. She pulled these on and then retrieved a dry pair of pants, socks and underwear. When she glanced up, Natalia saw one of the men in front, head turned as he watched her in near darkness. "Do you mind?" she asked in English. He didn't answer, or look away. Another of the men reached back and pulled a curtain across between them, giving her some privacy. Natalia took off her shoes and wet pants. With her dry clothes on, she tucked her legs up to her chest and wrapped her arms around her knees, so exhausted that sleep called to her, but Natalia could not take that chance. She was far too vulnerable. Instead, she rocked back and forth, trying to stay awake until they reached their destination, wherever that might be.

It was early morning when the van stopped moving. Still awake but completely exhausted, Natalia didn't react until the curtain separating her from the front seat was suddenly yanked open. The van's driver, a man with dark hair and a scraggly beard, climbed into the back and reached around her to open a side door. "Out," he said. The two other men still sat in the front seat, staring back at her vacantly. In the light of day, she saw them clearly for the first time. One was just a kid, rail thin and not more than fifteen years old. The one who'd watched her the night before. The man beside him could have been his grandfather, with a wrinkled face and grey hair.

"Where we are?" Natalia quickly reached for her gun.

Instead of answering, the man tossed her duffel, clothes and hat out onto a dirt shoulder. "Go!" he shouted.

Natalia climbed out and the door slammed closed behind her. A few seconds later the van took off in a cloud of dust, leaving Natalia standing alone. Her wet clothes were covered with dirt but she put them inside the duffel and then zipped it closed. A few dusty shops lined the road. Behind these were large, brick apartment blocks. Fifty meters down to her left she saw a train station with a small crowd of commuters waiting on the platform. In the distance beyond was the sprawl of Istanbul. She was back. Rita was somewhere in this city. Natalia hoisted the bag on her shoulder and headed toward the station.

Chapter Thirty-Three

Aksaray was the last stop on the line. Natalia joined a crowd moving through a tunnel and then up a crumbling stairway. At the top she emerged into daylight and was engulfed by the chaos of the city. People scurried in all directions across a cracked concrete square. Cars, trucks and buses flowed over arched bridges and roadways on all sides, honking their horns and spewing exhaust. Towering gray buildings hemmed in all of the action. Natalia threaded her way off the square and across one of the pulsing thoroughfares. After a few blocks, she turned down a narrow side street, past vendors selling fruit, spices, fish and fried meats. "Sultana Hotel," read a faded sign hanging from a non-descript three-story building. Two stars. She pushed the door open and moved inside to find a cluttered desk crammed in beside a stairway. A bored-looking clerk glanced up from his newspaper.

"One room," Natalia said. "With bath."

"How many nights?"

"Two."

"Eighty Lira. Pay in advance." He turned a register toward her. "Sign here. I'll need to see a passport."

Natalia handed over her forged Russian passport and signed the name, Alexandra Petrova. She gave the man a hundred euro note and he pulled out a calculator to determine the exchange rate before handing back her change in Turkish lira. Next, he took a room key from a row of boxes on the wall and pointed up the stairs. "Third floor. Breakfast begins at 8:30 on the terrace. It is included." The clerk handed her the key. "Do you need help with your luggage?"

"No, thank you, but I'd like to have some clothes cleaned if that is possible."

"Of course."

She left her wet and filthy overcoat, jeans and shirt behind before heading up the stairs with her bag on one shoulder. The room was small but clean, with a full-sized bed, a small desk in one corner, and a window facing the street. She locked the door behind her, tossed her duffel on the bed and went to look out the window. Directly beneath her was a faded red awning. Perfect if she needed to make a quick escape. A hop out the window and she could roll right onto the sidewalk, as long as the awning held. Natalia pulled the curtains closed and moved back to the bed. She reached over to flip on a light switch and then looked inside the duffel, pulling out the Kalashnikov AKS-74U submachine gun with attached GP-5 grenade launcher. She unfolded the stock and held the weapon in her hands. It felt comfortable after weeks of practice. She looked at herself in a full-length mirror holding the gun, the innocence of her life on the farm so very far away. Natalia knew firsthand the evil that lurked in the hearts of men. She also knew what an AKS-74U submachine gun was and how to use it. Even more importantly, she was prepared to do so.

Natalia folded the stock and put the gun away, her thoughts turning to her sister, here in this same city, terrified, her own naiveté being violently stolen away. Gregor's words ran through her mind. Don't rush things, he'd said. This was hard advice to follow. She wanted to head straight to the brothel and bust down the door. It was the kind of foolhardy impulse that could get her into trouble. Natalia was hungry and exhausted. By all rights she should be collapsing on the bed, but it was adrenaline that kept her going. When that adrenaline ran out, she knew she could crash. That would mean impaired decision making, a loss of focus and slowed reflexes. In short, quite possibly the difference between success and failure. It was better to eat something, to rest, and to formulate a plan. She should wait until the following dawn, when business was slow and the guards were sleepy. She hated leaving Rita there for a minute more than she had to, but Natalia would play it smart. She took the Glock from the small of her back and placed it on the desk. Slowly she took off all of her clothes and made her way into the bathroom where she turned on the shower, waited for the water to heat up and then climbed in, the warm, soothing stream banishing the chills from her cold, wet journey.

When she'd emerged once more from the shower and dried herself, Natalia slid her jeans back on and found her last dry shirt. She took her hat and rinsed it clean in the bathroom sink before hanging it to dry. Back in the bedroom she pushed the duffle to one side and lay down on the bed to rest. The clock on the table read 9:15 a.m. Twenty-one hours until dawn. Twenty-one hours to wait and to worry while Rita was at their mercy. She tried to clear her mind. She tried to sleep, rolling over from one side to another. After ten minutes, Natalia realized that despite her best intentions, she simply didn't have the patience to stay put in this room. Somewhere Rita was waiting. The time had come to find her.

Natalia rose again, considering which weapons to bring along. The machine gun seemed too bulky and obvious for this job. In close quarters the pistol would be sufficient. She lifted the Glock from the desk and released the magazine, checking it over before sliding it back into place. This time she tucked it into her waist at the front, pulling on a sweatshirt to hide the bulge. She retrieved a silencer from the duffel, slid it into her front pocket and then walked out of the room and down the stairs.

Outside on the street, Natalia blended into the crowd, pulling the hood from her sweatshirt up over her head as she started on her way, back to where her nightmare began. Zigic himself was unlikely to be there. That was a problem she'd have to solve later. Right now, finding Rita was all that mattered. She tried to channel her fear, picturing in her mind what needed to be done; forcing herself into the apartment, killing the guards if she had to, getting in and out as quickly as she could. By the time she rounded the corner onto that fateful street, Natalia was fueled by nervous energy. Any worries about a post-adrenaline crash were long gone, but she hoped she wasn't overlooking anything obvious. She thought of Gregor, trying to divine some additional wisdom he might have shared, knowing that once it began, everything would come down to instincts. "All right, you bastard," she muttered under her breath. "I hope you trained me well."

When she arrived at the building, Natalia stood staring at the buzzer on the door. Just a door like any other. Just a buzzer. But if she pushed it they might call down on the intercom. They might ask who it was. Before she considered this for long, the door opened and two young men stumbled out, laughing. They turned to Natalia in surprise and said a few words in Turkish. Natalia ignored them, brushing past as she moved inside. She closed the door quietly and moved on up the stairs, gun in hand. By the time she reached the second floor, she smelled cigarette smoke. Was it the guard? Sitting just outside the brothel door? If so, this might be his very last cigarette. She pulled the silencer from her pocket and screwed it into place.

When Natalia reached the fourth floor, she stopped. The guard would be just above her. There could be no hesitation. She preferred not to shoot him if she didn't have to, but if he went for his gun there would be no choice. She was ready. Up the stairs she went, bursting around the corner with her pistol pointed straight ahead. The landing was empty.

Natalia took a deep breath and knocked loudly on the door three times, holding a thumb over the peephole. If they didn't open up, she'd shoot her way in.

"Orada kim?!" came an unfamiliar woman's voice.

"Zigic sent me!" Natalia answered. There was a pause, and then a reply.

"Ne istiyorsun?" the woman said.

"Zigic!" Natalia repeated firmly. "He sent me to see you!" The bolt slid open. As soon as the door began to move Natalia stepped back and kicked hard with her right foot before pushing her way through to find the elderly woman sprawled on the floor. She was short and round, with long grey hair. Nobody else was in sight. No guards, no girls. No couches even. Natalia moved down the hallway, flinging open the door to Tanya's room. It was empty, both of people and furniture. She continued from room to room, finding the same each time. Aside from the one old woman, the place seemed to be deserted. Cleaned out. In Ludmilla's room, she finally found some furniture, along with an old man peering up at her from the bed. He was alone. "Where is Zigic?!" Natalia shouted. "Zigic!"

The woman pushed her way into the room with a fist in the air, hollering undecipherable obscenities. Natalia lowered her gun and tilted her head back, a sense of defeat washing over her. This place was her only connection to Zigic, and thus to Rita. "Zigic?" she said again to the man, but she was met with a blank stare. Natalia opened the drawers to Ludmilla's old desk one at a time. Save for a few paperclips and some blank envelopes they were empty. She turned to go, walking down the hall as the woman berated her all the way out the front door.

On the way back to the hotel, Natalia's mind went in a thousand directions at once. If this old couple did know Zigic, they would certainly tell him what had happened. From this point on he'd be expecting her. But where was he? More importantly, where was Rita? She looked up at the apartment buildings rising above her in all directions. In a city of 18 million people, her sister could be almost anywhere at all.

Chapter Thirty-Four

Natalia wandered the streets, looking into the faces of all those she passed. Had any of these people laid their eyes on Rita? As she was shuttled from a car and into seclusion? Natalia felt lost and dejected. She'd come to the city with no plan beyond returning to her own site of confinement. Now she had nothing to go on. The best sources of information were bound to be the women on the street, so she continued to wander, looking for prospects. Somebody had to know where Zigic was, but who could she ask? Around and around she went, from one block to another until finally she found herself taking a path to Marina's place.

From across the street, Natalia eyed the balcony where she'd spent those cold autumn evenings just six months before. It seemed like a lifetime ago. If anyone could help her, though, it was Marina. She knew the goings-on in this dark underworld as well as almost anybody. Natalia walked across and pushed the button beside the front door, waiting until a tired-sounding voice crackled over the intercom.

"Yes?" the voice said.

"Marina?"

"This is Marina. Who is this?"

"It's me! Natalia Nicolaeva!"

"Natalia?! But how?..."

"Can't I come in?" The buzzer sounded and Natalia pushed her way into the foyer. Her spirits lifted just a little bit with each step that she took toward the second floor. When she reached the apartment she found the door ajar, but Natalia knocked lightly anyway. "Hello?"

"Come in," Marina replied.

Something was wrong. Natalia could sense it even before she went through the door. When she stepped inside, all of the curtains were drawn and a smell of sickness and spoiled food permeated the air. Marina sat on the edge of her bed, pale and thin, struggling in an effort to stand. She'd aged a year or more for each of the six months since they had parted.

"Oh, my," Natalia gasped, hurrying to Marina's side. She knelt down on one knee as she took her friend's hand. "You should be in bed."

"What are you doing here?! Natalia! This is quite a surprise."

"You need to lie down, Marina!"

"I'd rather sit up and have some tea. Why don't you put the water on and then you can tell me all about why you've come back."

"Of course." Natalia tried to hide her concern.

"Perhaps you could help me to the table?"

Natalia took Marina's elbow and guided her across the room. "Are you warm enough?" Natalia lowered Marina into a chair.

"Yes, thank you," Marina answered, but Natalia found a shawl in the bureau for her anyway. She draped it over Marina's shoulders and then turned to the kitchen, filling the kettle with water. Cockroaches scurried across a pile of dirty dishes in the sink.

"I'm sorry the place is such a mess," Marina croaked. "If I'd known you were coming…"

"How long have you been this way?" Natalia placed the electric kettle in its cradle.

"Oh, not long."

"How long is that, exactly?"

Marina didn't want to answer. "Let's not talk about me. Tell me why you're here?! I can't imagine you've come back to work again? Not my Natalia!"

"I think you know me better than that."

"Yes, I suppose so." Marina avoided Natalia's eyes.

"Don't ignore my question, Marina. How long is not long? I want the truth."

Marina sighed. "I don't' want you to worry about me."

"I *am* worried. I have every right to be!"

"It's just a flu, I'll be over it in a few days."

Natalia sat in a chair on the opposite side of the table. This was no flu. Anybody could see that. Marina's gaunt features, the state of her apartment, the weight loss. Whatever it was, she'd been fighting it for weeks if not months. "Have you seen a doctor?"

"I don't need a doctor!"

"What's wrong with doctors?" Natalia took Marina's hand in her own once more.

"Please, Natalia!" Marina pulled her hand away. "Tell me why you're here. It isn't to pester me, I'm sure of that."

Natalia leaned back in her chair, stung by Marina's rebuke. Why the secrecy? And how could Marina expect to get better if she wouldn't even accept the concern of a friend? Maybe that was just it. Maybe she didn't expect to get any better. Perhaps she'd simply given up; surrendered to whatever disease was stalking her. "I'm not trying to pester you," Natalia said.

"Tell me some good news, then. Tell me you're here on vacation this time. Or that you've met a man. Some wealthy business-type, taking you on a world tour."

"No. I'm afraid it's nothing of the sort. I'm here to find my sister."

"Your sister?" Marina repeated the words. "Why your sister? You can't mean, after all you went through…"

"Zigic came for me. Or some of his men did, anyway. I wasn't home, so they took Rita instead."

"Oh, Natalia!"

"I've come to get her back."

"But…" Marina struggled to process this information.

"I went to the apartment but nobody was there," Natalia continued. "Just an elderly couple. I couldn't even speak to them."

"Natalia, you know what they will do if they find you!"

At this mere suggestion, Natalia's eyes burned with an intensity that only hatred could inspire. "Not this time. Things are different. They're the ones who should be worried."

"You got away with it once, but…" Marina was dumbfounded. "You're talking about taking on an entire criminal gang, by yourself? Do you know how that sounds?"

"I'm not here to entertain doubts. I'd appreciate it you kept yours to yourself." Natalia found took out some tea bags and put one in each of two mugs. When the water boiled, she lifted the kettle from its cradle.

"You've changed, Natalia. You're not the same girl I knew before."

"They killed my father. They stole my sister. They made me a pariah in my own home town. Even my fiancé turned against me. There is nothing I won't do to make them pay for what they've done." Natalia poured the water and then brought the mugs to the table. "I'd hoped you might be able to help me."

"Of course," said Marina. "You know I'd do anything for you."

"Can you tell me where he is? Goran Zigic? Have you heard anything about him lately?"

Marina still couldn't hide her concern. "You know he's very well protected."

"Please…"

"I'm sorry." Marina put both hands on the table in front of her. "Hand me the city map, from the bookcase."

Natalia moved across to a set of shelves cluttered with books and papers, stuffed animals and souvenirs. "Where is it?"

"Third shelf, left side."

Natalia found the map and brought it over, unfolding it across the table.

"I heard he's opened a club. It's called *The Blue Room*. Some of his girls work there." Marina pointed to a spot on the map. "We're here," she said. "*The Blue Room* is here, on Guvenlik Caddesi. You might find him there, but Natalia, I wouldn't go. It's not safe for you. Maybe the police will help you this time."

"I have to go, Marina. I have to do this on my own. Don't worry, I can take care of myself."

Chapter Thirty-Five

The walk from Marina's apartment to Guvenlik Caddesi wound through a labyrinth of narrow, winding streets, over crumbling sidewalks and past decaying five-story buildings. When Natalia finally found *The Blue Room*, the door was closed and locked. She took a few steps backwards and looked up at the apartment windows above. There were no signs of life. Zigic's girls had to be close by, but figuring out where exactly would take some work. Even then, there was no guarantee that Rita would be among this group. If these girls did work for Zigic, though, they might know something. Natalia would come back later, when the club was open. Sleep still called out to her, but she couldn't give in quite yet.

On the way back to Marina's place, Natalia walked around the neighborhood several times, familiarizing herself with the layout. She stopped at a small market along the way and picked up some fruit, cans of soup and two loaves of bread. Marina was too sick to go to the market herself, and nearly out of food. She'd been surviving on a dwindling bag of rice and some canned vegetables. It seemed that Natalia had shown up just in time. She didn't want to picture it, but the image of Marina starving to death all alone in that small apartment was hard to shake. When Natalia got back, she opened one of the cans and poured the soup into a pot on the stove. She turned on the burner and then set about cleaning the pile of dirty dishes.

"You don't have to do that," Marina protested from her place in bed, but there was no enthusiasm in her complaint. She was resigned to whatever help she might get.

"You relax," Natalia replied. "First I'm going to feed you and then we'll give you a bath."

"Thank you, Natalia," Marina conceded. Her relief was palpable. "I haven't had one of those in a while."

"I'm going to take care of you, Marina. All you have to do is let me, though it might help if told me what was wrong with you."

"Don't worry, it's not contagious. Not in the usual sense."

"So you've seen a doctor?"

Marina couldn't, or wouldn't, answer this question.

"Come on, Marina, talk to me!" Natalia pleaded.

"Yes, I've seen a doctor…" Marina's voice trailed away.

"And what did the doctor say?"

"What I've got is a hazard of the trade."

"You tested positive," Natalia put it together. "How long have you known?"

"A year. Maybe more."

"A year!? And you kept working?!"

"What was I supposed to do? A girl has to survive!"

"But I was here… And you didn't say anything?!"

"Would it have made a difference?"

Natalia stirred the soup. "There are drugs, you know. People lead long healthy lives!"

"Do you know how much those cost? I have no papers here. I can't even see a doctor unless I pay. I was on those drugs for a while but… business has been slow."

"There must be someone that can help you. Some organization? You can't just give up like this, I won't let you!"

Marina didn't have the strength to argue. "I am glad you're here, Natalia. I want you to know that. You're the closest thing to family that I have."

For Natalia, this was perhaps the saddest part of it all, that someone could be so alone in the world. She turned off the burner and ladled the soup into two bowls, then sliced the bread and placed it on a plate on the table. "Come, let's get some food into you."

Once Marina was fed, bathed and tucked back into bed, clean and warm, Natalia left the apartment and took a streetcar toward the waterfront. She needed some time to clear her mind, to prepare herself for the night ahead. Clinging to an overhead strap as the tram lurched and jolted down the track, Natalia was bumped and pressed on all sides. Through the windows she saw minarets reaching for the sky, shopkeepers sitting in front of their stores and tourists lounging in sidewalk cafes. The streetcar wound down past Topkapi Palace to the docks, where Natalia climbed out and joined throngs of workers, rushing to catch their ferries home at the end of the work day.

At a railing along the water, crowds of men held long fishing poles over the bay, bouncing their lines up and down as they tried to catch their dinner. Natalia gazed across the Golden Horn and on up the Bosporus Strait. She watched the fishing boats, ferry boats and cargo ships plying the water in a mad and complicated dance. Far across the waterway she spotted a large white ferry, the size of a cruise ship with a big blue smokestack. Giant blue letters across the side read UKR FERRY. The same ship she and Sonia arrived on the previous spring, so full of hopes and dreams. Natalia wondered how many girls arrived each week with similar expectations. She couldn't stop the trade, that was impossible, but she could make a dent. She could kill Zigic. This idea was becoming an obsession.

Continuing through a pedestrian tunnel under a large bridge span, Natalia emerged in a small concrete amphitheater overlooking the bay. Groups of locals sat idly chatting on the steps, an island of calm in a tempestuous city. Natalia found a place of her own and sat to watch the sky turn a golden yellow in the west. She inhaled deeply, the salt air filling her lungs. Nearby she spotted a young couple, giddy with euphoria. This was what happiness looked like, she thought. That sensation was a luxury she couldn't afford. Hers was a cruel and heartless world, yet still there were moments. Returning to the farm to see her family. Time spent with Gregor. Her last night in Drosti, falling asleep in his arms. Even in a life with so much pain, there still was joy to be found. Natalia took in the buzz of this city all around her and made a silent pledge. When all of this was over she would create a life for herself somewhere out in the world; in London or Paris or Rome, or perhaps even that small, quaint fishing village on the Italian coast. She would succeed on her own terms, if not for herself alone than for Sonia, too. She would live this dream for both of them. But first, she had a sister to find. Natalia turned and walked back the way she had come, desperate for just a few hours of sleep.

Chapter Thirty-Six

From a clear plastic bag, Natalia pulled out three wigs, one at a time, and placed them on the bathroom counter before her. She'd slept for two hours, crashing so hard that the alarm almost didn't wake her. Even after rousing herself and taking another shower Natalia still felt groggy. She did her best to focus on her task at hand. The first wig was blond and shoulder-length, the second long, straight and dark, and finally the one she was searching for; short, black and curly. She tried this third one on, tucking her own hair underneath as she looked into the mirror, turning her head from side to side. She had a long way to go. From another bag, Natalia sorted through a selection of rubber noses and chins, cheeks and a black moustache. She made room for them on the counter as well, along with application glues and matching foundation. It took more than an hour to blend her new face together, but even with the elements in place, something wasn't right. Her eyebrows were long and thin. They ought to be bushy. She dug through her kit until she found what she needed. She had to give Gregor credit. He thought of everything. Natalia pulled off the adhesive backing and applied the eyebrows. It was a big improvement. When she looked in the mirror, Natalia saw a man's face staring back.

Using scissors to cut a bathroom towel into squares, Natalia taped them to her shoulders before putting on her overcoat and adjusting it in the mirror. Loose pants hid her feminine legs. Black leather boots provided the final touch. It was all in the presentation, he'd told her. If you believed it enough yourself, you could pass for anyone. Natalia tried hard to believe it. She stuck the pistol in her coat pocket and headed out the door. When she got to the ground floor, she moved past the front desk and out before the clerk could say a word. Once on the street, she tried to gauge the reaction of passersby. Nobody paid her any particular attention. That in itself was a good sign. She lifted her shoulders and forged ahead, trying her best to walk like a man. That part shouldn't be so hard, she thought. According to Gregor, she always walked like a man…

It was still early when she arrived at *The Blue Room*. Business wasn't likely to pick up until sometime after midnight. Outside on a stool, a burly doorman sat lazily watching the activity on the street. He gave Natalia the once-over as she approached but didn't say a word when she walked on through the door. Inside, a stairway led straight down. Natalia followed it, her anxiety mounting. At the bottom, she emerged in a long, narrow room. A bar ran along one side and a dance floor the other. A disco beat throbbed through the air, with squares of colored light bouncing off the walls. On a row of barstools, a middle-aged man sat beside two blonde girls in tight skirts. Nearby, a bartender cleaned beer glasses, looking up as Natalia walked in. Across the dance floor, three more girls smoked cigarettes, talking amongst themselves. All three watched Natalia as she walked in, though they didn't seem particularly concerned. Natalia tried to identify them in the dim light but none looked familiar. One was tall, thin and slightly awkward. She stood with arms crossed in a frayed denim skirt and white halter-top, looking over as Natalia took a seat at the bar. A plump girl with short dark hair and heavy makeup commented to her colleagues and looked away. The third girl had an average build, with pink hair and a black leather skirt and top. She barely paid attention to Natalia at all.

When the bartender approached, Natalia merely pointed to a beer tap and raised one finger in the air, afraid to speak lest she give herself away. Even her woman's fingers might have blown her cover, but the bartender didn't seem to notice. He filled a half-liter glass and placed it on the bar before her. "Thirty euros," he said. Natalia's eyes opened wide but she pulled some of Multinovic's bills from her pocket and dropped the money on the counter. By the time she turned around, the three girls from across room were on her.

"Hello, mister," said the plump one in heavily accented English. "Having good time?"

"Buy us a drink?" said the tall one.

Natalia shook her head no, but the girls paid her no heed. "Champagne," the plump one said to the bartender.

"Nyet!!!" Natalia growled in a deep voice. "I pay for my drink. Not theirs."

The bartender gave this some consideration before crossing his arms and looking to the girls. The tall one shrugged and the three of them walked back to the other side of the room, ignoring Natalia once again. She took a small sip of beer. At these prices, she'd have to make it last.

Before long, another pair of customers appeared at the bottom of the stairs, taking their places at the far end of the bar. In the next thirty minutes, a few more men dribbled in and more women as well, from a separate door in the back. Some stood along the wall while others sat in chairs arranged for them. A few flirted more directly, hitting the men up for drinks and attention. Nobody danced.

After they'd had a few drinks, some of the men began to choose. One nodded his head to the tall girl, who led him through the door and into the back. A few others followed suit. Natalia knew she had to get back there. Rita might be somewhere behind that door. At the very least, Natalia needed to get one of these girls alone, where she could ask some questions in private. Steeling herself to the task, she stood and walked across the room, stopping in front of the pink-haired girl. Without a word, the girl nodded and led Natalia toward the back. They went on through the door, past a man who sat dozing in a wooden chair. Natalia nearly froze. It was Oleg, the same pale, skinny man who'd guarded the door at the apartment. He jerked his head abruptly when the girl kicked his foot. "Number five," he mumbled, hardly noticing Natalia at all. They continued past and on down a corridor, Natalia following the girl into one of the rooms.

"One hundred euros." The girl closed the door behind them. "In advance."

"I need some information," Natalia said in Russian, making no attempt this time to disguise her voice.

"What is this?!" The girl moved two steps back, staring at Natalia in awe.

"I just need to ask you some questions," Natalia continued.

"Who are you? The police?"

"No," Natalia answered. "I'm not the police."

"I'm registered, you can check for yourself."

"I told you, I'm not the police! I'm looking for another girl. A girl named Rita. Do you know her?"

"Of course I know Rita. I know three girls named Rita."

"This Rita is new. She would have just arrived within the last few days."

"Why are you bothering me about it?" The girl was growing angry.

"I need some help. Please. Have you seen her?"

"You're going to get me into trouble." The girl moved toward the door.

"Rita is my sister!" Natalia pleaded. "Please! She's only sixteen!"

The girl stopped and crossed her arms. "You owe me one hundred euros. Pay up or I'll call security."

Natalia dug the money from her pocket. "Why won't you help me?"

The girl snatched the bills from Natalia's fingers and stuck it in her bra, folding her arms once again. "Why should I?"

"Why are you here?"

"Because all the good jobs were taken. Why do you think?"

"My sister was kidnapped by these people. She was stolen right out of our home. They shot my father dead, right in the front of her."

"Then you know what they'd do to me if they hear us talking!"

"All I need is some information…" Natalia implored her. "Is there anything you can tell me? Anything at all? I'll pay you, if that's what you want!"

"Shh! Quiet!" The girl paused, weighing her guilt against the consequences of being caught. "Tomorrow. Be at the Laleli tram stop at noon. I'll talk to you then."

"You promise?"

"I'm not promising anything." The girl reached for the door handle and bolted out of the room. Natalia followed, past an oblivious Oleg and on into the disco. She took one last look at the other girls, scanning unsuccessfully for familiar faces. She cast her eyes along the bar, hoping for a sight of Zigic himself, but the man was nowhere to be seen. For now there was nothing left to do. She walked back up the stairs, shuddering as she made it safely to the street.

Natalia walked half a block and found a place to sit in the stairway of an apartment building. She backed up into the shadows to watch and wait. From here at least she could see the entrance to *The Blue Room*. If Zigic arrived, she'd know. She could also watch the girls on the street, and the touts wandering up and back, trolling for business. If she was observant, perhaps she'd pick up some clues; maybe spot some of Zigic's men coming from one of the apartment buildings up and down the block. She settled in to wait with a back against the wall. The longer she sat, though, the harder it was to fight off her exhaustion. Her eyes dipped closed. Her body slumped to one side. Consciousness ebbed... Just before she toppled over, Natalia jerked herself awake, sitting straight and tall. She tried to revive herself, shaking her head back and forth and then focusing on the comings and goings on the sidewalk below. Minutes later, she was nodding off again. It was no use. Natalia struggled to her feet and stumbled back in the direction of her hotel. She would get some desperately-needed sleep and then meet the pink-haired girl at the tram stop the following day. Natalia hadn't found Rita yet, but at least she was making some progress. That was what she tried to tell herself, anyway.

Chapter Thirty-Seven

After a fitful night of sleep, Natalia sat on a bench at the tram stop, rocking nervously back and forth. The cars came and went, passengers hopping on and off, going about their daily lives with no conception of this underbelly of existence in which she and Rita were trapped. Natalia looked at her watch. It was already ten minutes past noon. She had a sinking feeling. The girl wasn't coming. There was no reason Natalia should have expected her to, yet the disappointment went straight to her core. Days were passing and she seemed no closer to finding her sister at all. This connection with the pink-haired girl was looking like just another dead end. But then she saw another girl approaching. Someone familiar, coming straight toward her along the platform. This girl had blond hair, long and straight. She wore a white leather skirt and matching jacket with strappy high-heeled shoes. Could it be?

"Hello, Natalia." The girl stood before her. "I thought it must be you."

"Helena!" Natalia was aghast as she looked her old acquaintance up and down. "You're still working for him?!"

"I paid off my debts. I earn good money now," said Helena. "Tanya was right about one thing. I guess you get used to it."

"What about your modeling? What about Milan? And Paris?"

"I didn't come here for a lecture." Helena's cheeks turned red.

"It's not a lecture, Helena! I thought you had plans?"

"Plans change."

"What about your fiancé? Don't you want to get married? What about your future?"

"Natalia, if you keep this up I'll walk away."

Natalia swallowed hard. She couldn't squander this opportunity for a view to the inside. "Why did you come to see me anyway?"

"I heard Irina talking. I knew it must be you. Who else? But I had to see for myself, just to be sure."

"The girl with the pink hair?"

"You can forget about her, she's not coming. All she wanted to do was get rid of you."

Natalia no longer cared about Irina. Surely Helena must know something. "You haven't seen her, have you?" Natalia asked. "My sister, Rita?"

"No. I haven't seen her." Helena took a seat on the bench beside Natalia. "But I might have heard a few things."

"What things?"

"Do you know the name Adnan Kemal?"

"No. Who is he?"

"A very rich man. One of the wealthiest in the country. They say he has a thing for virgins. Apparently Zigic is holding a new girl for him. A virgin. For his birthday."

"Where is this girl? What do you know about her?!" Natalia couldn't hide her alarm. This had to be Rita. It must be.

"All I know is that Kemal's birthday is today. He's throwing a party at his house. If it is your sister we're talking about, you'd need a small army to get her out."

"Where is the house?" Natalia demanded. "Have you seen it?"

"Yes. I was there once. The house is on the Bosporus. On the Asian side."

"Can you show me?" Natalia pulled Marina's city map from her pocket and unfolded it across her lap.

"What are you going to do?" Helena was worried.

"Just show me, please?" Natalia begged.

After a moment's hesitation, Helena looked to the map. "It was somewhere near here," she pointed. "Not far from the Vanikoy ferry dock. You can see the bridge from his back patio. I don't know what you'll do about it, though. Kemal has his own private security force. You can't just stab one man and get away like you did the last time."

"Tell me about the house. The layout, how many guards he has, where the master bedroom is located. Tell me about this man, Kemal. What does he look like? Does he have any other family? Any eccentricities?"

"Natalia, you're making me nervous."

"Why don't you just leave this place? You, me, Rita... When this is all over, why don't you come with us?"

"And go where? Back to my parents' house?!"

"Is it so terrible?"

"They think I'm a model now. They think I'm rich and famous. What would I tell them?"

"Why not the truth?"

"Is that what you did? Did you tell your mother? And how did she take it?!"

Helena was right about that much. Just thinking about it now, Natalia felt the shame all over again; the disapproving stares of the townspeople, the clucking of the old women's tongues. "No. I didn't tell them," she admitted. "But somehow they knew. Everybody knew."

"I just need to earn some more money. Enough to be proud when I go back, so they'll believe that I've made something of myself."

"And how much money is that?"

Helena pushed the map aside and rose to her feet. "Look, I've told you where to find your sister, let's just leave it at that."

"Don't go, Helena! I'm sorry. Can't you tell me a little bit more about the house?"

"Honestly, I don't even want to be seen with you…"

"My friend's apartment isn't far away. Besides, I think you should meet her."

"I've risked enough just coming here."

"Please, Helena. We girls need to stick together. Can't you see that? What happened to the old Helena? The Helena I knew before? The one with some fight in her? Is the fight all gone? Have you given up completely?"

"Who said I'd given up at all?"

"But haven't you?"

Helena's eyes took on a glassy cast.

"I'm sorry," said Natalia. "I didn't mean to upset you. I shouldn't have said that."

Helena wiped at one of her eyes. "It only hurts because it's true."

"So help me then," Natalia urged her. "Show me you've got some fight left in you."

Helena nodded slowly. "All right. I'll tell you what I can."

Chapter Thirty-Eight

The local ferry was nearly empty as it plied the darkened waters of the Bosporus. Natalia stood at the rail in her skin-tight red dress, steadying herself atop her matching stilettos. Her hair was shoulder-length and blond; another of her carefully crafted wigs. In one hand she held a black leather purse, feeling the hard outline of her Glock inside. She stood tall and proud, playing the role of a confident, self-assured woman as they sailed past mansions of the Turkish elite. Hidden within swirled a mixture of apprehension and rage. Natalia's beautiful, innocent little sister was being given away as an offering to the god of wealth and power. Natalia did her best to focus that rage, for as dangerous as it might be if left unchecked, it was also a source of strength. It would allow her to do things she might not otherwise be able to do, acting as a counterweight to her fear.

Natalia heard the party before she saw it. Music mixed with the sounds of conversation and laughter drifted across the water. As the ferry drew close she saw an enormous two-story home, just as Helena had described, with faux-Greek columns, an outdoor swimming pool and a massive yacht tied up to a private dock. Guests gathered in tuxedoes and fancy gowns on the patio, serenaded by a live band. Atop the yacht, a tuxedoed man with a bushy black moustache stood between two women. The man's eyes locked onto Natalia as the ferry moved past. His were the eyes of a hunter, unconcerned at being caught in the act of devouring his prey. Kemal. Natalia dared not release her gaze. This was her adversary. She couldn't back down. Not now, not ever. The ferry moved on until his figure shrank away.

At the next stop, Natalia was the only passenger to disembark. Deckhands watched with sad eyes as she shimmied down the gangway. The boat pulled away from the pier, leaving her all alone in the dark of night. Natalia reached down to take off her stilettos. Under a pale sliver of moon she began to walk, purse in one hand and shoes in the other.

As she made her way down the road past waterfront mansions, Natalia thought over her strategy. She was counting on the dress and heels gaining her entry to the party. It seemed unlikely that the guards would turn her away. What worried her more was whether they'd try to search her purse. No matter what, she couldn't let them. Once inside she'd get a drink at the bar and try not to attract any undue attention while she assessed the layout and security, then make her way upstairs and search from room to room, starting with the master suite. If Rita was in the house, Natalia would find her, but she'd have to think on her feet, making decisions quickly and wasting as little time as possible. She had to be ready, mentally, to deal with any unforeseen problems. Hesitation could mean the end of both her own life and her sister's. Natalia tried to calm herself. She had to maintain composure. Stay focused.

Coming up the road from behind her, Natalia heard the roar of a sports car approaching at high speed. Turning to look, she was caught in the headlights before the car flew by. She saw the brake lights flash and the car slowed and turned around. As it came back, Natalia knew she was being watched. The car crept past and then turned again, pulling to a stop beside her. The passenger side window slid down. Natalia peered inside. A young man gazed back. Not much more than a boy, really. He leaned close to the open window. Smooth face. Short black hair. "Bir gezinti mi?" he said, but Natalia merely stared back blankly. "English?" he tried again. "You speak English?"

"Yes, I speak English."

"Why you doing walking here in dark?"

"I am going to a party."

The boy reached across and opened the passenger door. "Get in. We go same place."

Natalia did a quick appraisal. She could walk to the party, appearing by herself from out of the darkness and try to talk her way in as she'd planned, or she could pull up in style with an escort. She climbed into the car, sinking into the contoured leather seat, and pulled the door closed.

"Where you walk from?" he asked.

"The ferry."

"Ferry! Ha!" He revved the engine and took off down the road, throwing Natalia backwards. "You like my car? I just get it."

"Yes." Natalia gripped tightly to the door handle. "Very nice car."

"Where you from? From Russia?"

"Yes. From Russia."

"How come you not with a man?" he asked.

"How come you are not with a woman?" she countered.

"Now I am!" When the boy smiled, Natalia saw the glow of his white teeth.

Kemal's mansion was in sight up ahead, bathed in light. The boy slammed on his brakes and pressed a button on the car's sun shade. The front gates swung wide and he drove on through, past two security guards in dark suits. "What is your name?" he asked her.

"Sophia."

"I call you Natasha. We call girls like you Natasha."

"Ok, I am Natasha."

"Good," said the boy. "I am Yashar Kemal."

"Kemal?"

"Yes. My father's house."

He drove past a row of Mercedes, Jaguars and Porsches, pulling around a giant fountain and stopping in front of a wide stairway leading to the mansion's front door. Natalia looked to the upstairs windows. Rita was here somewhere. She could feel it. When Yashar stopped the car, two tuxedoed attendants rushed forward, one for each door. Natalia and Yashar climbed out and took a better look at one another as he walked around the front of the car. He was thin and gangly. Probably about 17 years old, she figured, with a loopy smile on his face as though he couldn't quite believe his luck. The car, she saw in the light for the first time, was a yellow Ferrari.

"Welcome to our home, Natasha."

"Thank you." Natalia forced a smile herself and then leaned down to put on her shoes. When she stood back up, Yashar offered an arm. In her heels she was a good 5 centimeters taller than he was. Natalia took his arm and together they climbed the stairs where a stocky security guard in a dark suit nodded deferentially. A doorman in a white jacket pulled open the front door. So far so good, Natalia thought, still clutching her purse. They entered a round foyer with a grand staircase wrapping up along the right wall. Moving on past, they entered a giant living room with a vaulted ceiling and second-floor indoor balconies on three sides. Massive windows faced onto the patio, the swimming pool and ships plying the strait beyond.

Guests gathered inside and out while uniformed waiters flitted amongst them, filling glasses and offering small delicacies on silver trays. Yashar led Natalia across the room and out onto the patio. So far he'd asked her nothing about who she was or what she was doing at his father's party. Apparently girls like were the norm, no explanation necessary. He probably didn't care, as long as he could exert some claim upon her. A few guests danced to the live music while others gathered around the pool. Most of them were men and women doing their best to age gracefully with expensive clothing, fancy jewelry and an aura of wealth and privilege that Natalia had never encountered before. Her eyes came to rest on Kemal, who had moved from the boat to a table on the patio where he held court with a small knot of men drinking cocktails and smoking cigars. A bulky security guard hovered close by, his eyes constantly moving, wary of any possible threat. Two more guards were positioned on the corners of the property. Lounging on some patio furniture near the water, Natalia spotted a younger set of guests, a boy and two girls. The boy waved a hand in the air and rose to his feet. "Yashar!" he shouted.

"My friends!" said Yashar eagerly, putting a hand on Natalia's back as they moved across the yard. When they'd approached, Yashar grasped his friend's hand firmly and wrapped an arm around his back in a masculine show of affection. "Ahmet!" he said.

The girls remained seated. "Sonunda yapti," said one of them as she looked Natalia up and down, making little effort to hide her derision.

"This is Natasha," said Yashar. "She speaks English."

"But no Turkish?" said Ahmet. He was short and thin, with dark hair and an easy-going air.

"No," said Natalia. "No Turkish."

"Ok, we speak English. Please, sit!"

Natalia took an empty chair next to the other girls, careful to face the party so that she could see who came and went. Zigic might show up. Or even Rita, though they'd never parade her in front of the other guests. If she were here at all she'd be locked away somewhere, out of sight. Natalia eyed a balcony that stretched above the pool on the second floor. She knew from her conversation with Helena that this was the master bedroom. The lights were off. She looked back to Kemal. As long as he was in her sights, Rita's honor was temporarily secure, but time was not on Natalia's side.

Yashar flagged down a server and procured two glasses of sparkling wine, handing one to Natalia. "Welcome!" he said.

Natalia smiled and touched her glass to his, gazing into Yashar's eyes before taking a sip. "Thank you."

"What brings you to our country?" Ahmet asked.

"Excuse me?" Natalia turned toward him.

"Why have you come to Turkey?" The slight smile on Ahmet's lips gave away that he already knew. Or thought he did, anyway.

"I am a tourist," Natalia answered.

"I see. And how do you find our country?"

"On the map!" Yashar gave a hearty laugh.

"Pardon my countryman and his weak sense of humor," said Ahmet.

"Why you are here at this party?" One of the girls came straight to the point.

"She is my date!" said Yashar.

The girl lowered a stinging gaze, first at Yashar and then at Natalia before rising to her feet and stalking off. Her friend quickly followed.

"Is there a problem?" Natalia asked.

"No, no problem." Yashar took a seat beside her and placed a hand on Natalia's thigh. She let the hand rest there, fighting the urge to push it away. When she looked back toward Kemal, he was staring directly at her from across the patio, as though she were already a part of his property, just like the house or the yacht. As though anything in his purview was his for the taking and Natalia especially. Their eyes stayed locked together as he excused himself from his guests and moved toward her.

"Father!" Yashar took his hand from Natalia's thigh and rose as the senior Kemal approached.

"You come to my party without saying hello?!" Kemal admonished his son.

"Happy birthday, father." Yashar embraced his father.

"And who is your friend?" Kemal eyed Natalia.

"Natasha," said Yashar.

"Natasha, welcome to my home." Kemal took her hand in his and bowed slightly as he kissed her fingers.

"Thank you," Natalia answered with a light smile, the hair standing on the back of her neck. Over his right shoulder she saw the light come on in the master bedroom.

"My son has excellent taste in women," said Kemal.

"You have a beautiful home." Natalia tried to maintain her composure. Upstairs the lights in the bedroom switched back off.

"Thank you very much," Kemal answered. "I would like to give you a tour."

"I will give her tour!" Yashar reached out eagerly to take her hand. Natalia grasped his fingers and stood.

"As you wish." Kemal was mildly perturbed. He leaned close and whispered into Natalia's ear, "But I will see you later." It was a command and not a suggestion. Natalia moved away with Yashar, back across the patio and on inside, eager to escape from Kemal's sight.

"I show you best room in house!" Yashar escorted her through the living room and down a long corridor, through double wooden doors to an interior room with a pool table on one side and large couches on the other. A massive TV screen was mounted to the wall. Yashar turned on the monitor and picked up a remote. He sat on the couch and loaded a video game. "Come, sit!" he said.

Natalia stayed where she was while Yashar lifted a controller and loaded a game. She watched for a minute or two as he manipulated a soldier running through trenches and blasting his enemies with a machine gun. "Bam! Bam! You dead!" he shouted with glee.

"Yashar!" said Natalia to no effect. "Yashar!" she raised her voice, moving between him and the screen.

"Hey, what you doing!?"

"Maybe you show me the rest of the house?" Natalia put her hands on her thighs. "Maybe you show me the bedroom?"

Yashar's face brightened. "Yes, of course, bedroom!" He hopped to his feet, tossing the controller aside. She followed him back through the doors and into the corridor. They turned right, away from the entryway. When they came to a smaller, back staircase, Yashar took her hand again and led her up. Natalia's senses were on high alert. With her free hand, she still held tightly to her purse. When they reached the second floor the hallway was empty. Yashar pulled her into the first room on the left. Posters of soccer players and half-naked women adorned the walls. On one side was an unmade bed. Dirty clothes littered the floor. "This is your room?" Natalia asked.

"Yes. You like?" Yashar flopped down on the bed.

"I would like to see your father's room."

"No. This is good room." Yashar patted the bedspread. "Come."

Natalia moved back into the hallway, unzipping her purse as she went. "I would like to see more."

"Hey where you go?!" Yashar called after, but Natalia kept moving, wrapping her fingers around the grip of her pistol. When a door to her right flew open, Natalia jumped backwards. A woman came out, laughing playfully as she went past. A man followed, barely glancing at Natalia before chasing the woman down the hall. Natalia moved to the doorway, peering inside. It was an office. Desk, computer, bookshelves lining the walls. Nobody else was there.

"Come back!" Yashar poked his head into the hall. "My room is good. Nice bed."

Natalia moved on, stopping at the next door. "What is inside here?"

"Bathroom," answered Yashar.

"Show me."

Yashar sighed deeply, resigning himself to her games. He padded down the hall and opened the door, standing aside so that she could see. "You need to use bathroom?"

Natalia flipped on a light switch and moved inside. Marble counter, twin sinks, large bathtub and a toilet, but no people. "I can show you guest room!" said Yashar with a hopeful smile. Natalia nodded and then followed him into another bedroom, this one clean and unoccupied, with a double bed in the middle and a dresser to one side.

"You will show me your father's room?" asked Natalia.

Yashar's frustration was evident in his pleading expression. He held his arms out by his sides. "But my father...!" he tried to explain.

"Please?" Natalia begged.

Yashar narrowed his eyes. "Ok. I show you room, but after we go to *my* room."

"Fine." If it came to that, Natalia could knock him unconscious and continue the search on her own.

Yashar approached a set of double doors. "My father's room." He turned a knob and pushed, then a step inside and switched on a light. Nobody was there. "You see? We go now."

Natalia moved past him into the room. On the left was a massive bed, cleanly made. Directly ahead, a set of curtains framed French doors leading to the balcony. Natalia made her way across and peeked through one of the window panes. She opened the door and walked onto the balcony, scanning the party below. The swimming pool was directly beneath her. Guests mingled around the edges, including Kemal who stood talking with two older gentlemen.

"You like view, yes?" said Yashar.

"Yes, very nice." Natalia saw Yashar's friends with a few other young people gathered on the yacht.

"We go to my room?"

"Later." Natalia could tell that his frustration was at a breaking point. "Yashar, I think you are very nice. A very nice boy."

"No," Yashar shook his head. "No, no, no. I no understand. You want money? I have money!" He took a wallet from his back pocket and pulled out a sheaf of bills. "Plenty money! Come, we go to my room!"

"No. I am sorry." Natalia peered back over the crowd, watching Kemal and the guards. "I must find someone."

"Find who?"

"My sister." Natalia looked Yashar straight in the eye.

"Your sister?! What her name?"

"Rita. Do you know Rita?"

"No, but I have money for her, too! She is beautiful, like you?"

"Listen to me, Yashar! I need to find her. She is with a man named Zigic."

Yashar's eyes lit up. "Ahhh...!" He broke into a smile. "Of course! Goran Zigic. A good man. Very nice."

"You know him?!"

"Of course! My father, they do business."

"What business?"

"Just business," said Yashar. "My father, he own phone company. Biggest in Turkey. And many other company, too."

"And Zigic?" Natalia continued. "Zigic sells ladies like me. So men can rape them."

"No, no rape." Yashar shook his head, suddenly looking very worried.

"Yes, rape," Natalia countered.

"For money yes, but no rape. Zigic is good man. This car I drive, this his car. He borrow me for tonight."

"Where is he now?!"

Yashar's eyes betrayed his suspicion as he weighed whether to tell her anything more at all.

"Yashar, won't you help me? Please?"

"I think you go, now," he replied, a young man scorned.

Natalia turned her attention back to the party below. "Not without my sister." Two beefy men in black suits walked out of the house and across the patio. One she recognized as the security guard from the front door. It was only when they stopped beside Kemal that the other man turned and Natalia caught a good look at his face. She recognized him, too. It was one of Zigic's men, less than twenty meters away. She dropped to her knees, hiding behind the balcony railing.

"What you are doing?" Yashar laughed uneasily, peering down at her in confusion.

"Shhh!" Natalia held a finger to her lips and then pulled the gun out of her purse and screwed on the silencer.

"Hey!" Yashar gasped excitedly. "You crazy?!"

"Quiet!" She pointed the gun at him. "Sit!"

"Look, you no shoot nobody!" Yashar raised his hands in the air.

"No. I don't shoot nobody. I get my sister and I go." Natalia held the gun in both hands. "She is here now."

"I go ask my father, ok? I find your sister," Yashar pleaded.

"Sit!" Natalia commanded again. He looked down below, weighing his options, but then lowered himself to a seated position not far away. From inside the bedroom, Natalia heard voices. She slid across the balcony until her back was against the wall beside the French doors. "Shhh, quiet," she whispered to Yashar and then motioned for him to slide back further out of sight. When he was off to one side, Natalia carefully peeked around the curtains. She saw three men, two with their backs turned. One had a suit cut a little bit nicer than the others. She recognized that suit and the man in it even without seeing his face. When he shifted to his right, Natalia saw Rita, hair in braids and wearing a school-girl's uniform; black leather shoes, dark stockings, green plaid skirt and a white blouse.

"What you will do?" whispered Yashar.

Again Natalia put a finger to her lips. The men inside spoke to each other in low tones. One walked toward the open balcony door and stopped just before the threshold, his attention distracted by the Bosporus beyond. Natalia's blood pressure rose. If the man took one more step he'd see them both sitting here, Natalia with a gun in her hands and Yashar cowering behind. Natalia held her breath. If she shot the first man, Zigic and the second might have time to pull their weapons. And if bullets started flying, Rita could get caught in the crossfire. The man near the doorway moved back into the room and Natalia breathed again. When she peeked inside once more, Zigic was pressing Rita against the bathroom door, one hand grasping her thigh. "You'll be a good girl, tonight, won't you?"

Natalia knew she had to make a move. There would be no better opportunity. She slid off her shoes and took three quick breaths. In one swift movement she jumped to her feet and swung through the door, pointing her gun from one man to another and back in quick succession. "Don't move!!!" she shouted. "Hands where I can see them!" She'd caught them by surprise and their expressions showed it.

"Unbelievable!" Zigic and the others raised their hands in the air, though he had a bemused look on his face.

"Na, Na... Natalia?" Rita sputtered in disbelief

"You think this is funny!" Natalia said to Zigic.

"Oh, Natalia..." Zigic gave her a bitter smile as he shook his head. "Did you like what my men did to your father? I will do the same to you, and your sister, and your mother and everyone you ever knew!"

"You are in no position to make threats," Natalia spat back. Despite his bravado, she was sure she detected a hint of fear in his eyes. It was an emotion she'd never seen in him before, but he was worried, that much was clear.

"Put the gun down and I might spare your mother," said Zigic. "I may only rape her."

The two henchmen had waited long enough. They went for their weapons, thrusting their hands under their jackets, but Natalia spun quickly and shot one in the head, the other twice in the chest. The men fell to the floor, their guns bouncing off the plush carpet. Zigic's arrogance vanished for good, the fear of God upon him in a flash. He pulled Rita close, nearly choking her with one arm as he tried to shield himself behind her. "Put the gun down!" Zigic held his free hand in the air, as though he could stop the bullets with his palm. "I'll break her neck!"

Natalia aimed her pistol at Zigic's head. "Let her go," she said calmly, but the gun shook in her hand, a testament to the power he still held over her.

"Look at you!" Zigic laughed in desperation. "A frightened little peasant girl!"

"I said let her go," Natalia repeated, watching the color drain from Rita's face as she gasped and squirmed in Zigic's clutches. If only she would hold still for a moment. If only Natalia's hand would stop shaking. She knew she could still make the shot; but what if she missed?

"Drop the gun like a good girl," said Zigic.

"You have five seconds!" Natalia shouted.

"Praise God!" Yashar bounded inside. "You shoot them!"

Natalia turned her head just a fraction, but it was a fraction too much. Zigic rushed forward, shoving Rita ahead of him like a battering ram. Natalia had no time to react as her sister slammed into her and they both went crashing to the floor. Rita rolled to one side and the next thing Natalia felt was Zigic's foot on her forearm, pinning her wrist to the ground. "Drop the gun!" He stood over her with his own weapon pointed at her face. Rita crawled backwards and away until she bumped into the wall. Natalia opened her fingers and let her pistol fall free.

"My father, he not going to like this," said Yashar. "No, not like."

"Shut up and take her gun!" Zigic shouted.

Yashar bent down and retrieved the Glock. "What you will do?"

Zigic lifted his foot from her forearm and took one step backwards, keeping his gun trained on Natalia's forehead. She still saw the fear in him. Multinovic was right. Underneath his usual swagger, Zigic was a coward after all. This knowledge was power to Natalia. Despite her predicament, she knew she could beat him. Her heart swelled with confidence. Zigic looked anxiously to the two dead men and Natalia recognized her moment. She spun herself around in a flash, wrapping her legs under Zigic's ankles like a vice and twisting her entire body in a roll to the left. Zigic reached out with both hands to steady himself but it was no use. He toppled like a falling tree, slamming into the floor with a violent explosion as his gun went off, blasting a hole in the bedroom wall. Natalia sprang to her feet, kicking him hard in the abdomen as Yashar backed away in terror. Zigic rolled onto his knees in an attempt to stand but Natalia caught him full-force between the legs and he crumpled into a fetal position, groaning in pain. One more kick to the head left him sprawled out unconscious on the floor.

From outside, Natalia heard the sound of men shouting. She turned back toward Yashar to find him standing three meters away, pointing Natalia's own gun at her.

"Put the gun down!" commanded Natalia.

"You don't move!"

"I know you won't shoot me, Yashar. Just put the gun on the floor and step away!"

Yashar shook his head. "No." He placed his finger on the trigger.

"Yashar, that is a very dangerous weapon. I know you don't want to hurt anybody. Please!"

Again Yashar shook his head, bewilderment showing on his face. From outside, the shouting continued and Natalia heard footsteps charging up the stairs. She bolted to the bedroom door and turned the lock just in time before an unseen hand tried the knob from the other side. Yashar took two steps backwards.

"Rita, it's time for us to go." Natalia moved quickly to her sister, helping Rita to her feet as the men outside banged on the door. On the floor nearby, Zigic groaned as his consciousness slowly began to return. Natalia eyed his gun, a few feet away on the floor.

"Don't," said Yashar. "You no move."

Natalia kept her steely gaze on him as the two sisters walked past and out onto the balcony. The pounding on the bedroom door grew louder and more frenzied as the men outside tried to break it down. Yashar stayed where he was, frozen by indecision. "We're going over!" Natalia said to Rita.

Rita's eyes opened wide when she saw the pool directly beneath them. "I can't swim!" The banging at the door ceased for a brief moment followed by the sounds of gunshots blasting at the lock.

"It's time to learn!" Natalia lifted her sister around the waist and swung her legs up and over the rail. She heard a collective gasp from the horrified guests below as she released Rita who fell with a giant splash into the water. In the next moment, the bedroom door burst open and three of Kemal's men rushed into the room. Natalia saw Yashar, pointing toward the balcony. And she saw Zigic, halfway to his feet, his glazed eyes upon her. Natalia was next over the rail free-falling into the swimming pool, down through the water she went until her feet hit the bottom. Bending her knees, she pushed off with her legs and shot back upwards until she broke the surface. Natalia barely knew how to swim herself but thrashed her arms and legs in a desperate attempt to keep her head above water. Nearby was Rita, completely submerged. Natalia grasped her by the shirt and pulled her to the edge, managing to shove her up and part way out of the pool. Rita sputtered and coughed before scrambling the rest of the way out as the party guests moved further back and away. Kemal himself was nowhere in sight.

"Hareket ettirmeyin!" one of the men shouted down from the balcony. All three men pointed their guns at the two girls, though they seemed to be confused as they tried to figure out what was actually going on. Natalia pulled herself from the pool and then held her hands in the air to show that she was unarmed. "Ok, ok!" she yelled while quickly eyeing the escape route, through the house and on out. When she looked back up again, Zigic appeared at the rail, his own gun in hand. Natalia grasped Rita's arm and they sprinted inside to the ringing sound of gunshots and then screams as bullets ricocheted across concrete.

Through the living room they ran, past the giant staircase and out the front door. A parking attendant stood beside a board covered with keys on metal hooks. Natalia quickly ran her fingers over them, lifting off a set with a Ferrari symbol on the keychain. She pressed the alarm button and heard a chirping sound from the rows of cars on the lawn as the yellow Ferrari's lights flashed on and then off again. "Come on!" she shouted to her sister.

When they reached the car, Natalia opened the driver's door and bounded into the seat as Rita climbed in on the passenger side. Zigic and the other men raced out of the house after them, but it only took the push of a button for the engine to roar to life. Natalia punched the gas pedal and the car's back end spun out as she cranked the steering wheel to the right. Straightening it back out, they took off down the driveway, gravel flying through the air. The back window exploded as bullets riddled the car. "Keep your head down!" Natalia pressed the button on the sun shade and the front gates began to swing open. A lone security guard stood in the way, waving his hands back and forth. Natalia gunned the accelerator again and he dove aside, the Ferrari clipping the edges of the gates and bursting on through in a shower of sparks. The car skidded left, then swerved right as Natalia frantically turned the wheel one way and then the other until their momentum settled forward and they hurtled down the road and away, past darkened mansions, the ferry dock, and on into the urban sprawl that was Istanbul.

Chapter Thirty-Nine

They sat in the darkened Ferrari, parked behind a commercial building on the outskirts of the city. Rita trembled in Natalia's arms. "It's all right, we've made it," Natalia tried to soothe her. "It's all over." Natalia closed her eyes and buried her face in Rita's hair, inhaling deeply. "It's all over," she repeated the words, even as she knew they weren't true.

"I'm sorry, I'm so sorry," Rita cried.

Natalia leaned back in alarm. "What are *you* sorry for?"

"I didn't believe you. I should have believed. You tried to tell me…"

"Rita! You have nothing to be sorry for! You did nothing wrong!" Natalia put a hand on the side of her sister's face.

"It was just like you said."

"But I hardly said a thing. I was afraid to tell the truth."

"You told us they were bad men."

Natalia took Rita's hand. "They can't hurt you anymore."

"But Natalia, I wasn't the only one. There's another girl!"

"There are a lot of girls, Rita. I'm sorry, but we can't save them all."

"But we can't just leave her there! Alina is locked in a cage, just like I was!"

"Where?" Even with firsthand knowledge of Goran Zigic's depravity, this news shook Natalia.

"I don't know, in the basement of a house."

"Whose house? Where is this house?"

"I don't know! The man with the beard. I think it was his house."

"Zigic."

"We have to tell somebody. We have to call the police!"

"We can't call the police."

"But we have to tell *somebody*!" Rita's voice quivered with desperation.

Natalia turned her attention to a touch screen on the dash, pushing a button to initiate the onboard navigation system. "Where would you like to go?" a woman's voice asked in English.

"Home," said Natalia, noting the irony of the word. The path to their own home led first through his.

"Turn right, now," said the voice.

"What are we going to do?"

"I'm going to take care of it." Natalia hit the car's ignition switch. The engine came to life with a low rumble and Natalia drove around the building. "I'm sorry, Rita, but there's nobody else who can help us." She turned right onto the highway.

"Left turn toward Bosporus Bridge in 100 meters," said the voice. Rita sank back in her seat, as if trying to disappear. Natalia kept to the speed limit, hoping to attract as little attention as possible while driving in a bright yellow V-12 Ferrari with a broken rear window and crumpled front bumper. She knew the car was likely equipped with a tracking device. She also knew she'd be wanted for murder. Double homicide. The police might close in at any moment. "Turn left toward Bosporus Bridge."

When they'd crossed the bridge, the navigation system led them down winding roads and up a hill into a neighborhood of enormous homes. A high brick wall stretched along the road on the left side. As they approached a large metal gate Rita tensed up, afraid to move, afraid to even breathe.

"You have arrived at your destination," said the navigation system.

"You recognize this place?" Natalia asked.

Rita nodded, eyes wide.

Natalia drove past slowly. Through the gate she saw a large round driveway and beyond that, a large two-story house with a solid-looking wooden door. A black SUV was parked in front, along with a sleek black Mercedes that Natalia recognized. Light shone from a window upstairs but Natalia saw no signs of life. She continued on past without stopping. "How do you get into the basement?"

"There's a door, through the kitchen," said Rita. "But you can't just go in there!"

"Does this door have a lock?"

"Yes."

"What kind of lock? Do you need a key to get in?"

"There's a keypad. You need the code."

Coming after Zigic was part of Natalia's plan all along and now she knew exactly where to find him. Rescuing this other girl was just another wrinkle. "I have to take you somewhere for safe-keeping," she said.

"And then you'll come back?"

"Yes, then I'll come back."

"But what if *he's* here?"

"I'm counting on it." Natalia turned the car around and drove back down the hill, scanning for any signs of police as she went. On through Istanbul, Natalia made her way to the city center where she pulled into an underground parking garage. She found a space far in a back corner, hidden as much as possible behind a larger sedan. As soon as she climbed from the car, Natalia immediately noticed the surveillance cameras. They didn't really matter as long as she stayed one step ahead. The authorities could know where she'd been, as long as they didn't know where she was going. Rita followed her up the stairs to street-level and then down two blocks to the hotel. In her room, Natalia's duffel was packed and waiting on the bed. She slung it over her arm and they were out of the room in seconds. The front-desk clerk said nothing as they hurried past and out the front door.

They'd walked only a block down the sidewalk when they heard the high-pitched whine of sirens approaching at full speed. Natalia pulled Rita into a darkened alleyway as two police cars flew past, lights flashing, and then screeched to a halt outside the parking garage. An officer opened his door and crouched behind it, pointing his gun toward the entrance.

"We'll go the other way," Natalia whispered before leading Rita down the alley. They turned right at the next intersection and made a broad detour down quiet side streets all the way to Marina's place. Natalia rang the bell, looking around to see if they'd been noticed by anyone at all. No other pedestrians were in sight. When the door buzzed, Natalia pushed on through, pausing on the other side to catch her breath as the door swung shut behind them. They made their way upstairs, where Marina was back in bed by the time they entered the apartment.

"You brought me a visitor," Marina croaked.

"This is Rita." Natalia dropped her bag on the floor and closed the apartment door. She moved across the room to pull the curtains shut as well.

"You did it." Marina's relief was evident. "I thought I'd seen the last of you."

"I'm glad you had such faith in me," Natalia replied.

Marina ignored the comment and turned her gaze to Rita, who stood near the door, unsure of herself. "So young," said Marina. "And so beautiful. Come in, come in! Forgive me for not getting up. I'm Marina."

Rita smiled uneasily and moved further into the room, finally taking a seat at the dining table.

"Did you kill him this time?" Marina asked Natalia.

"No," Natalia replied. "Not yet."

"*Not yet*?! You're not planning to go back?!"

"I have to. You know that I do."

Marina was disturbed. "And you'll leave your sister for me to take care of? Is that it?"

"I won't be gone long. A few hours at most."

"Why don't you quit while you're ahead?! You've got your sister back!"

"You know there's more to it than that."

"You want your revenge. That's what this is about."

"No!" Natalia snapped. "It's not about revenge! It's about getting my life back! It's about never again having to look over my shoulder!"

"You want to see him suffer. To grovel at your feet! You're letting emotion cloud your judgment. This isn't some game you're playing!"

"I don't need you to tell me that," Natalia seethed. "You're not the one who lost a best friend. Who lost a father! You're not the one who can't sleep at night, knowing that he might come for you, for everyone you love, at any time. I can't live like that! I won't!"

Marina looked down toward her hands, struggling to find an answer to this attack. "All of us have had to endure our fair share of pain."

At this, Natalia felt a wave of regret wash over her. She moved closer to Marina and sat, taking one of her friend's hands in her own. "I'm sorry. I shouldn't have said those things. It was selfish."

"I worry about you, Natalia. That's all."

"I know you do." Natalia did want to see fear in Zigic's eyes, and yes, maybe even a hint of remorse if that was possible. Marina was right about that. "I'll be as careful as I can be. Come, let's have something to eat." Natalia took two cans down from the cabinet and looked toward Rita. "I hope soup is all right. It's about all we have."

"There's a bit of bread left as well," Marina added.

"Why don't you take care of this, Rita, I'd like to have a shower." Natalia put the cans on the counter along with a can opener and a pot. "After I get out maybe you can tell me something more about the layout of Zigic's house. Anything you remember at all."

"You're just like mother, you know," said a misty-eyed Rita. "Strong as a bull and just as obstinate."

"What about Alina? I thought you wanted me to rescue her."

"I want the police to rescue her. You can't do this yourself, Natalia. You'll only end up getting killed!"

Natalia crossed her arms. She couldn't argue with her sister over this one. The truth was, she very well might get killed. In fact, it was probably more likely than not, but Natalia was willing to take her chances. Goran Zigic must die, and Natalia was the only one for the job.

Rita moved to the counter and picked up one of the cans. "Go ahead and take your shower. The soup will be ready when you're done."

Without another word, Natalia retreated to the bathroom. She turned on the tap and pulled the dress off over her head, throwing it onto a chair. Next she slid the bobby pins out of her wig and took it off, running a hand through her natural hair before rolling off her stockings and underwear and stepping into the shower. The warm water caressed her face and ran down the length of her body. She'd killed two more men. All life was precious, she knew, yet for these men she felt no pity. Live by the gun, die by the gun. Just one year ago the thought of taking a human life would have seemed preposterous, but she was hardened now and chalking up a tally. Natalia tried to relax and clear her mind. This battle was not yet over. She must be prepared for the finish. By morning it would be done, one way or another.

Chapter Forty

The taxi cab slowed as it passed along the high brick wall fifty meters from Zigic's front gate. "Here!" Natalia called out. "You can drop me right here." The driver pulled to the side of the road. Natalia paid the fare and climbed out with her duffle bag, the strap heavy on her shoulder. She wore her full-length grey coat, jeans and black boots. Her long hair was tied tightly at the back of her head. When the taxi pulled away she was alone on the roadway, illuminated from above by a single streetlight. She ducked under a tree and into darkness before dropping her bag to the ground and pulling open the zipper.

The first thing Natalia took from the duffel was a bullet-proof vest. She removed her coat and fastened the vest tightly around herself, then put the coat back on over the top. Next, she retrieved the submachine gun, with grenade launcher attached. She felt through the bag with one hand until she found two 30-round magazines, loading one into the gun and putting the other into a pocket. She shoved the small stash of grenades into her other pockets one at a time, loading the last grenade into the chamber itself before strapping the gun across her back. A hunting knife went on her right calf. Lastly, she took out a lump of C-4 explosive, two blasting caps, two lengths of fuse and a lighter. The empty duffel she bunched up and shoved under a bush.

Natalia walked toward the front gate. On the other side, the same two cars were in the drive. Above and behind, a figure paced back and forth in an upstairs window. Zigic? She couldn't be sure.

There was no sign of any guards, though she knew they were there, lurking someplace out of view. A surveillance camera pointed toward the gate. Another took in the yard. The top of the brick wall was lined with razor-sharp pieces of broken glass, a low-tech way to keep out intruders. It made no difference to Natalia. She wasn't going for a quiet entrance. She would announce her arrival, the louder the better. Zigic was afraid of incoming fire? Then let him piss in his pants. Natalia pulled out one of her blasting caps and stuck in a four-inch length of fuse. She put the cap in her mouth and bit down carefully, crimping the metal around the fuse and remembering Multinovic's words about careless terrorists blowing their faces off. When she tugged on the fuse it was tight and her face was still intact.

Natalia did a quick appraisal, estimating the weak spots on the gate, the distance to the house, and the likelihood of return fire coming from the windows. If she hit them hard and fast, they'd have little time to respond. She had to be careful, but she couldn't over think it either. Natalia pulled out her small brick of C4. At the side of the gate, she mashed her putty around one of the hinges. She stuck in the blasting cap, pulled out her lighter and lit the fuse before moving along the brick wall and crouching low. A thunderous explosion shook the ground and everything around her, nearly knocking Natalia over. She regained her bearings and moved back through billowing smoke to find the gate askew, still connected by the top hinge, but with an opening at the bottom. Natalia slid through, raising her weapon as she rushed the front door. An angry black swirl of motion flew toward her from the left. Natalia fired a short burst and a Rottweiler dropped dead at her feet.

From inside, Natalia heard commotion, voices shouting, feet pounding. She cocked her grenade launcher and fired, blowing the front door backwards off its hinges. Advancing forward she saw a man sprawled underneath, immobile. She moved past and inside.

To the left was another door, and a large fireplace beyond. To the right, a stairway leading upwards. Natalia saw muzzle flashes from a landing at the top and darted left through the doorway as a hail of bullets rained down from above. She felt no fear, only adrenaline and a rising fury. She wanted these men dead. A deep desire for vengeance overtook her. Not just for herself, or her sister, but for all of them. Helena, Victoria, Sonia. Every girl who'd ever been enslaved by men like these. Men who offered no mercy and thus deserved none in return. The time had come to pay their due. To answer for their sins. She was the one who would *make* them pay.

Natalia poked her head around the corner and saw a man with a pistol, crouched low between the stairway railings. The muzzle flashed again and she heard bullets slam into a strip of molding just above her head, splintering the wood into chips. She ducked back, unscathed, knowing he wouldn't likely miss again. From her knees, she blindly held her gun around the corner and fired off three short bursts but there was little chance she'd hit a target that she couldn't see. Instead, Natalia pulled the gun back, loaded another grenade and rose to her feet. Holding the gun tightly, she counted down from three and lunged around the corner, firing her grenade at the dark crouching figure. Two bullets crashed into her chest, throwing her backwards. Natalia gasped for breath and scrambled for cover as the grenade exploded in a ferocious blast. On hands and knees, she pulled open her jacket and examined the slugs embedded in her vest, front and center. Loosening the straps, she inhaled deeply three times before daring to take another peek at her assailant. This time she saw the man's crumpled body, inert at the bottom of the stairs, a pool of blood spreading slowly across the floor. He was finished. The same with the man still lifeless under the shattered front door. Two down. How many guards were left? Natalia had no idea. She released the first magazine from her gun, not wanting to run out at an inopportune moment, and fished in her pocket for the fresh one before locking it into place.

Natalia moved quickly, past the two dead bodies and on up the debris-littered stairs, senses straining for any signs of danger. Was that the sound of a door closing? She couldn't be sure. When she reached the second floor, she walked down a hallway and charged into the first room on her left. It was the room she'd seen a figure in earlier, standing near the window. The light was still on. Cigar smoke hung in the air but the room was empty. She checked under a desk and behind a couch. Nobody. Just the abandoned cigar, still burning in an ashtray on the desk.

Back in the hallway, Natalia moved to the next door, gently trying the handle this time. This door was locked. Taking a step backwards, she kicked as hard as she could with the bottom of her boot but the door wouldn't budge. She fired three shots at the lock and the door swung open. Natalia knew that someone had locked it from the inside. It had to be Zigic, hiding himself away. She burst through the door, gun blazing away at a mirror and artwork and a giant TV on the wall. Lamps and windows shattered and the furniture was ripped to shreds. Nobody was there. She checked under an empty bed and down beside a dresser. Inside a wardrobe she found only bullet-riddled clothing. She searched a small attached bathroom. Nothing. There was only one other place he could possibly be. From behind a closet door she heard a man's choked sobbing and then some unintelligible mumbling. He was talking to himself. Praying? Natalia couldn't tell. She pressed herself against the wall to one side. "Come out, Zigic," she said.

He answered her with gunshots, as bullets blasted through the door, whizzing harmlessly past. One grenade would end it, she thought. Or a quick burst from her machine gun. Instead, she reached a hand over to the doorknob and gave it a gentle turn. She wanted to see his face in these final moments. She wanted him to beg forgiveness, for ruining her life, for stealing her sister, for killing her best friend. For having her father murdered in cold blood. And besides, somebody had to let her into the basement. With her finger tight on the trigger, she used the barrel of her gun to slowly open the door. Inside Zigic sat on the floor, pistol in hand. When he saw the gun pointed inches from his forehead his expression went from fear to amusement and back again as he struggled to comprehend reality.

"It's you!" He laughed to himself before tossing his pistol away. "You won't shoot me! Not an unarmed man!"

Despite what Multinovic had told her, Natalia still marveled at how pathetic Zigic had become. This was her monster. The source of so many nightmares was just a sad and broken man. She still yearned to empty her clip into his gut; to see his body jump and shake as the lead tore him to pieces. There would be time for that later. "Get up!" she shouted.

"Ok! Ok!" Zigic waved his hands in the air.

Natalia moved backwards but kept the gun trained on Zigic's head as he rose, trembling, to his feet. She nodded toward the hall. "Let's go. Out!" she commanded. "And keep your hands in the air."

Zigic narrowed his red, bloodshot eyes as he walked out the door. "Where are you taking me?"

"We're going to get Alina." Natalia stayed a few steps behind him as he walked along the hall and turned down the stairs.

"Who?"

"Just keep moving."

At the bottom of the stairs, Zigic saw the two dead bodyguards. "What do you want, Natalia?" he pleaded. "You can have anything! You can run one of the houses. You can run them all. You'll earn big money. *Big money!* Buy cars and a house. It is a good life, Natalia. I promise you!"

"The basement!" Natalia shouted. "Now!!!"

"Ok, the basement. I will show you the basement," Zigic mumbled. They turned right and he led her through a kitchen with two oversized ovens, gas stoves and a large center island.

"Keep your hands on top of your head," said Natalia as they passed out through the other side of the kitchen and turned a corner, coming to a small door directly underneath the stairs. It was solid steel, with an electronic keypad to one side. Just like Rita had told her. "Open it."

"How can I open it with my hands on my head?"

Natalia pressed her gun barrel to the base of his skull. "I said open it." Zigic lowered one hand and pressed a code into the keypad. A green light flashed and Natalia heard the lock click open. "You first," she said. "Slowly."

Zigic pulled open the door and flipped a switch, illuminating a narrow stairway. He descended downwards with Natalia close behind. The stairs led into a damp, brick cellar. On the far side were two steel cages, each of them roughly two-meters square. Lying on a cot inside one of them was a girl, wide-eyed and silent, huddled under a thin blanket.

"Alina?" said Natalia. "It's ok, I'm here for you."

In a quick flash of movement, Zigic lunged toward the wall and the lights went off, plunging them into total darkness. Natalia fired her gun but it was too late. Zigic's hand was on the barrel, shoving it up and away as he wrenched the weapon from her grasp. Natalia fell to the floor. Pushing herself backwards, she saw quick flashes of light and felt the hot lead of a single bullet tear through her right calf, clipping the leather sheath that held her knife.

"Where are you, bitch?!" Zigic growled. Natalia reached down with one hand and pulled out the knife, sticky with warm blood. She held it in the air, arm cocked, waiting. The lights came on, Zigic standing with one finger on the switch. Natalia hurled the knife toward his head. The heavy metal handle struck Zigic hard in the temple, sending him to the floor in a clump, out cold. Natalia scrambled to her feet and reached for the gun, pulling it out from under his motionless body.

"Alina?!" Natalia turned to the girl in the cage.

Still huddled under her blanket, a shocked Alina managed a nod.

"You're going home," Natalia added. "But you have to tell me, where is the key?"

Alina raised a shaky finger and pointed to a hook on the wall. Natalia grabbed the key ring and quickly moved across to the cage. When she'd opened the door, she helped Alina up and then out, barefoot and dressed in only thin underwear.

"Stand aside." Natalia let go of Alina, lifted Zigic's limp body by the arms and dragged him into the cage before moving back out and locking the door behind him. He wasn't dead yet, but he would be soon enough. Through the bars, she kicked at his foot until he opened his eyes and looked up at her.

"How does it feel?" she said to him. "Being locked in a cage?"

Zigic thrust an arm toward her, but Natalia jumped backwards just out of reach. He pulled his arm back into the cage and climbed to his feet. He was dazed, as though he couldn't quite believe what was happening. Natalia stood facing him. This was it. After wanting to kill this man for so long, the time had finally come. It almost seemed too easy, watching him there completely helpless with no recourse but to die. Natalia wasn't about to feel any pity. She would give him the mercy he deserved. None at all. She gripped the gun tightly, pointed it at his body and squeezed the trigger. Nothing happened. She tried again, but still the same. A demented smile crept across Zigic's lips and he started to laugh. Natalia held the gun up and examined it. She tried to release the clip but it wouldn't come out. It was bent. She banged on it with her hand and tried again but it was no use.

"I knew you wouldn't shoot me!" Zigic was full of mirth and glee. "You can't kill me! Not some useless whore like you, Natalia. That's all you are. Don't you ever forget that! You're a whore!"

"Come on, we're leaving." Natalia took Alina by the hand.

Zigic lunged at the cage again and then grabbed the bars, rattling them back and forth. "I will get you for this!"

"Your threats are hollow now." Natalia led Alina back up the stairs and into the kitchen. At the first stove, Natalia lifted the cover and leaned close to blow out the pilot. She did the same for the oven and then followed these steps on the second oven and stove. She turned all of the knobs to full and held her breath as the room began filling with gas.

"Let's go," she gasped to Alina, leading her quickly into the entryway. Sticking up from a small hole the floor beside the fireplace was a metal key. Natalia turned it to the left until she heard an unmistakable hissing sound. She and Alina ran out the front door and across the yard. Near the gate, Natalia stopped and turned to face the house. It was over. She'd done it. Almost. Lifting her gun once more, she fired a grenade it into the window of the SUV. The car blew up into a ball of flames, waves of heat licking at their faces. Natalia did the same to the Mercedes and then turned toward the house.

"We should go," said Alina, the first words she'd managed.

"In a minute," said Natalia. By now the gas would be making its way through the open basement door and down the stairs, filling the space where Zigic sat trapped like a rat in a cage, breathing the fumes, desperate to escape. Only this time, there was no escape. Natalia loaded her last grenade and fired it through a kitchen window. Seconds later the entire house erupted in a massive explosion, orange and yellow flames leaping through shattered glass, a concussive shockwave knocking them both to the ground as debris rained down around them.

Head ringing, Natalia climbed back up. "Are you all right?" she asked Alina, who managed a furtive nod as Natalia helped her to her feet. Natalia took off her long grey coat and draped it over Alina's shoulders. "Now we can go." She paused to take one last look at the house. Thick black smoke poured from every door and window. If anybody inside could have survived the explosion, there was no way they would live through the fire. At long last, Natalia was free. She threw her gun to the ground and they ducked through the shattered gate. Natalia tore off her bulletproof vest as they walked off down the street, back toward lives left behind.

Chapter Forty-One

The farm lay sprawled before them as they came over the rise, smoke wafting upwards from the chimney of the main house. It all looked the same, tucked in below rolling hills, as though nothing at all had changed. When the Lada drew close, the children's faces appeared in one window. Moments later they raced outside with Olga in tow. Ivanka pulled the car to a stop. As soon as Natalia climbed out she found a child clinging to each leg. "Natalia! Natalia! Natalia!" they cried out in unison.

"What about me?" Rita emerged from the passenger door.

"Rita! Rita!" shouted the children, rushing around to greet her next.

Olga stood by with a look of joyous disbelief. "You made it."

"Yes, we made it," said Natalia.

"And we brought a friend with us, too!" said Rita.

In the back seat, Marina sat wrapped in a blanket with a soft smile on her face. "Hello," she nodded to Olga through an open door. "I'm Marina."

"Marina is going to stay with us," said Rita.

"Come, let's get her into the house!" said Ivanka. She helped Marina out of the car and up the steps as Natalia took their bags from the trunk. Before they were unloaded, another familiar face emerged from the barn. Natalia froze where she was, hardly able to believe her eyes. It was her long-lost brother Leon. Hair trimmed and neat, face clean shaven. He walked across the yard and stopped to face Natalia just a few feet away.

"It's really you." Natalia couldn't hide her astonishment. She turned to her mother. "Why didn't you tell me?"

"I thought it would be a nice surprise," Ivanka replied.

"But how...?" Natalia was practically speechless.

"I heard about father."

"Are you're going to stay?" Rita asked.

"Yes. I'm going to stay." He pulled the last bag from the trunk.

Natalia dropped her own bag and grabbed him in an embrace. She had so many questions for him. Leon was home, he was sober and he seemed to be at peace. That in itself was miracle enough. Questions could come later.

"What did you bring us, what did you bring us?" sang the children.

"Come now, that's not polite!" Olga scolded them, though Natalia had never seen her sister-in-law so happy. She had her husband back.

"I brought you a kick in the pants!" Natalia said to the children as she let her brother go.

"Aw, that's no fun," Valery pouted.

"I'll tell you what; I'll bake a nice big cake. How does that sound?" said Rita.

"Yay! Cake!" said Valery, skipping up the stairs and into the house.

When they'd cleared the dinner dishes from the table, the early evening sun still shone through the windows. Natalia paused near the kitchen sill to look outside. The snow was long gone and the hills were covered in a carpet of fresh green grass. Spring had arrived in earnest. The planting season. She saw fresh furrows in the fields. Beside the barn, the tractor was hitched to the plow. "Where is father?" Natalia turned to her mother at the sink.

"At the top of the hill," answered Ivanka as she washed the dishes. "So he could be near us."

"That's good," said Natalia. "He'd prefer it that way."

"Your friend Gregor came to the service. I was wrong about that man. I tried to give his money back, but he told me to keep it. He said it was for you."

"I'll take it back to him tomorrow," said Natalia.

"No. He is gone," said Ivanka.

"Gone, where?!"

"I don't know. He packed his truck and drove away. I don't think he's coming back. That's what people are saying."

Natalia looked back out the window. She never even got to tell him that she made it. He'd have been so proud of her…

"Where is the cake? We want cake!" cried the children, crowding in the kitchen doorway.

"Only good little girls and boys get cake!" shouted Rita, chasing them through the door and around the house as they giggled with glee.

Natalia moved to the sink and picked up a towel, drying the dishes one by one and then stacking them on the counter. When she was finished, she moved back to the dining area and lifted an orange flower from a vase on the table. "I'd like to go see father." Without another word, she walked on out the door.

The sky was pale yellow as Natalia climbed the hill behind the house in the cool evening air, the temperature dropping as the sun dipped below the horizon. She'd walked this path countless times over the course of her life, to sit on the knoll and reflect, or read a book, or smoke her very first cigarette. This time she felt a hollowness inside. She was weak in the knees, afraid to face her father. Afraid that he might blame her somehow for everything that had happened. She felt him there, before she'd even crested the hill, as though he'd been waiting, his presence heavy around her. At the very top, amid the green shoots of spring, a fresh mound of dirt touched up against a headstone, carved in wood and bearing her father's name. Natalia knelt low, placed her flower on the grave and then sat down beside it. From here she could see the entire farm stretching off into the distance. She inhaled earth and manure and grass; smells her father knew so well. She picked up a handful of soil from his grave and squeezed it tightly, letting the dirt fall through her fingers.

Surveying the scene below, the house, the barns, the animals, Natalia thought back to the girl she was before; so full of passion yet afraid to leave this familiarity behind. Indeed, her heart would always be anchored in this place, yet she'd changed in these last twelve months. Natalia knew that she could no longer stay here. It really was too small to contain her. Gregor was right about that. It was why he'd left the money behind, to give her a head start. At what, she couldn't quite say, but she'd have plenty of time to think about that. For now it didn't matter. For now, Natalia was home.

Printed in Great Britain
by Amazon